Amanda,
the Cut-up

**Other Apple paperbacks
you will enjoy:**

Hurricane Elaine
by Johanna Hurwitz

Aliens in the Family
by Margaret Mahy

Millicent the Magnificent
by Candice F. Ransom

Summer Stories
by Nola Thacker

Sixth Grade Secrets
by Louis Sachar

A Really Popular Girl
by Kathryn Ewing

Amanda, the Cut-up

Vivian Schurfranz

AN
APPLE
PAPERBACK

SCHOLASTIC INC.
New York Toronto London Auckland Sydney

ISBN 0-590-42555-2

12 11 10 9 8 7 6 5 4 3 2   0 1 2 3/9

Printed in the U.S.A.   40

First Scholastic printing, December 1989

1

Amanda Kingsley, with unbuttoned coat flapping and scarf flying, raced down the icy sidewalk. Her first day at Kennedy School and she was late, she thought with a panic. She hoped her sixth-grade history teacher was understanding. Breathing hard, she flung open the door and pitched into the long dark hall. All the doors were closed; not a student was in sight. Her boots made snow tracks on the gleaming tiled floor as she hurried to her locker. Why, oh, why had she gotten on the wrong bus and then had to transfer? Well, she thought, as she dashed past a row of lockers, no one could expect a small-town kid from Iowa to find her way around Evanston, a large suburb of Chicago, right away.

She stopped at locker 867, and with numbed fingers fumbled with the padlock. Between short breaths, she whispered, "Turn right to three, then left back to nine, and right to five." She pulled on the lock, but it still remained firmly shut. "Oh, no," she groaned in exasperation. Shakily she tried again, and this time the lock opened. Thrusting in her coat, scarf, and gloves, she yanked out five notebooks, one for each class, banged shut the metal door, and tore down the corridor. Fortunately yesterday afternoon, as soon as they'd arrived from Mason, Iowa, Amanda'd registered. Her counselor had given her a computer printout of her schedule. And as she raced along, she nervously peered at the room numbers until she reached room 111.

She smoothed back her red curls, but the wiry coils immediately sprang right back to their original position. Taking a deep breath, she opened the door and hesitantly entered the classroom. The room was pitch-black, and for a moment she stared into the darkness. Wasn't anyone there? Then she noticed a shaft of light beaming up on a screen.

"And this is the *Santa María*, Columbus's flagship," a petite student said as she turned the knob on the filmstrip projector.

Amanda stood still in the doorway, while light fell across the screen. "Come in, come in," the student said impatiently, "and close the door. What is it?"

"I — I'm Amanda Kingsley," Amanda said in a trembling voice as her eyes became accustomed to the gloom. Where was the teacher?

"Oh, yes," the voice replied, softening. "You're the new girl from Iowa. Have a seat right there in the corner until I can check you in."

Amanda was glad no one could see her cheeks flame. The "girl" running the projector was the teacher! Amanda turned suddenly and bumped into a desk, and before she knew it, her books and pencils crashed to the floor. She moaned inwardly, scooped up everything, and hurried to her desk. Already she'd made a terrible impression on — she squinted at her schedule for her teacher's name — on Ms. Novak. Well, this was history class, and if there was one subject Amanda was good at, it was history. When Ms. Novak saw how many facts she knew, she'd soon forgive her tardiness. She hoped. Shadowy faces loomed around her. What were they staring at? Yes, I'm the new girl, Amanda thought, wishing she could crawl under her desk. The boy across the aisle stared at her, and for a second their eyes met; then he hastily glanced back at the screen.

Well, she thought sourly, you'd all better get used to me. I'm here to stay. She was not beautiful, but she wasn't ugly, either. Sure, she had uncontrollable hair like orange-red wire coils that framed her lean face, and sure, she was too thin, with freckles that peppered her hollow cheeks, but she had other good features like a small nose and nice green eyes, fringed with long lashes.

But who could see her in the dark? She should relax.

When Ms. Novak finished the filmstrip, she asked Jonathan, the boy across from Amanda, to rewind the film and put the projector away. So that's who he is, Amanda thought. Jonathan. Nice name. When the lights went on, she saw that he was quite tall and almost as slender as she was. He had a pleasant round face that was topped with stubby black hair cropped in a crew cut. Maybe he was a swimmer. She was. It might give them something to talk about.

Ignoring the glances in her direction, Amanda concentrated on the writing on the blackboard. *Exploration Unit* was the heading on a chart of explorers, listing their nationality, what country they'd sailed for, and the date.

Ms. Novak, a petite young woman with short brown hair, smiled at Amanda. "Class, this is Amanda Kingsley from Mason, Iowa," she said pleasantly. "I hope everyone will go out of their way to help her find her classes today."

Everyone swiveled about in unison. They took another long look at the new girl while Amanda stared down at the colorless polish on her pink nails.

"What's your next class, Amanda?" Ms. Novak asked.

Amanda cleared her dry throat. "Science," she croaked.

"Who has science next period?"

A blonde girl raised her hand. "I do."

"Jessica, would you take Amanda with you up to 204?"

"Sure," Jessica said, flipping back her long silky hair and giving Amanda a brief smile. "No problem."

"Now, let's talk about the filmstrip we just saw," Ms. Novak said. For a few minutes she reviewed some of the major points and asked questions. Next she discussed Columbus's life, concluding with the statement, "Columbus died in 1503."

"Fifteen-oh-six," Amanda piped up, immediately wishing she could disappear. Whatever possessed her to correct a teacher on her first day in a new school? But she'd blurted out the right date before she could stop herself. Now all she could do was return Ms. Novak's openmouthed stare and feel the hot crimson creep from her face into her hair roots.

"Fifteen-oh-six?" Ms. Novak repeated coolly, raising her eyebrows. "Are you sure, Amanda?"

"Yes," Amanda said in a choked voice, feeling Ms. Novak's gray-blue eyes fasten on her.

"Why, class," Ms. Novak said with a forced

chuckle, "it seems we have a real history student among us, but let's check the date just to be certain." She tilted her pretty head. "William, will you get the encyclopedia?"

A large boy with shaggy brown hair nodded and lumbered over to the bookshelf. Pulling out the C book, he quickly flipped through the pages until he found the entry for Columbus. He glanced back at Amanda and a wide grin spread across his big face. "She's right, Ms. Novak," he said triumphantly. "Columbus died in 1506."

"Well," Ms. Novak said, obviously flustered, smoothing down her neat, short hair. "That's very good, Amanda, but we must remember that dates aren't too important. It's the overall sweep of history that we need to understand."

Amanda bit her underlip, glancing at the nearby door. She was so near that she wondered if she couldn't just slink out. But no, that was a crazy thought. Instead, she'd sit there, afraid to move or breath or say another word. Everyone must think she was Ms. Know-it-all!

Ms. Novak gave her a cool smile, then turned to the class, her smile warming considerably. "I'll give you the last ten minutes to begin reading tomorrow's assignment." She sat at her desk and said sweetly, "Amanda, come up so I may check out your textbook and give you an assignment sheet."

Amanda felt every eye focused on the back of her green sweater as she went up to the teacher's desk. She shuffled first on one foot, then the other, as Ms. Novak recorded her name in the grade book and filled in Amanda's ID number. Good thing she didn't write *Amanda Kingsley, the klutz who drops things and who's tardy and who corrects her teacher,* thought Amanda. I'll bet the story of the Iowa girl will be the main topic at lunch today, both with students and teachers.

"This book is expensive," Ms. Novak cautioned, "so be very careful with it." She handed the heavy book to Amanda, then recorded the number on a card.

Amanda looked at the fat volume, *Our Country's History.* What an imaginative title, she thought with a crooked smile.

"Write your name inside," Ms. Novak warned, "so that if it's lost someone can return it. You'll find all the necessary reading listed on this assignment sheet." She handed Amanda a piece of paper. "You'll have a lot of catching up to do."

Ms. Novak seemed almost glad about it, Amanda thought glumly, as she turned around and forced her wooden legs to carry her back to her seat. Some teachers would have been glad to have a mistake corrected, but Ms. Novak obviously wasn't one. She'd probably bear a grudge for the rest of the year.

"Amanda," Ms. Novak said, and Amanda wondered how such a small person could have such a penetrating voice. "Why were you late?"

Oh, no, Amanda thought, now everyone will know I was so dumb that I got on the wrong bus. "I — I caught the wrong bus," she stammered.

"I see," Ms. Novak replied, as if to say, "Well, the new girl might know her history, but otherwise she isn't too bright."

The kids must believe my face is this shade of scarlet permanently, Amanda thought. When the passing bell shrilled, she had never been so glad to hear a sound in her life.

Jessica came over to Amanda's desk and smiled. "Ready for science?" she asked.

"Not really," she answered with a tight little smile, gathering up her books and hoping she could hold on to them this time.

As they threaded their way through the crowded hall, Jessica called out to several students, constantly smiling at this one and waving at that one. She must be one of the most popular girls in school, Amanda thought wistfully as she walked upstairs with her. Why is it that some girls have everything? She stole a glance at the lovely girl beside her. Jessica, with golden hair and a perfect oval face, was not only beautiful but popular as well!

When they reached 204, Jessica said, "Here we

8

are," and she went straight to her desk, not lingering to talk. She was pleasant enough, Amanda thought, but she had her own friends and why should Jessica care about who Amanda was or where she came from? Amanda sighed. The day had scarcely begun, and already it was a disaster!

Well, she thought, standing by the door waiting for the teacher, last week she'd had lots of friends, too. With a pang she remembered Ann Crowley, her best friend in Mason. Ann, plump and always with a broad smile, had lived across the street and they'd shared everything. When they were little, it was dolls, paper dolls, kick-the-can, and hide-and-seek. Later it was baseball games and concerts in the park. A band tightened around Amanda's heart. How could she stand it in Evanston — a new place where she didn't know anyone and had already rubbed one of her teachers the wrong way? Tonight, she vowed, she'd write Ann a long letter. She didn't care if there were boxes to unpack and posters to hang.

"Amanda Kingsley?" A smiling man came racing into the classroom. He bobbed his head up and down at her. "I'm Mr. Poindexter. Why don't you sit here?" He indicated a front row seat. "Welcome to science class."

Amanda looked about at all the strange faces. This really was a huge school. Unlike in history class, at least she could see in this sunny room.

9

How grateful she was for a friendly teacher like Mr. Poindexter. She'd like to pat his bald head and say, "Thanks for being a good guy." Breathing a sigh of relief, she settled back. She might even like science better than history this year — if that were possible.

2

After her first week of school Amanda walked down Sycamore Street, thinking of her classes. Even though school wasn't quite the disaster of her first day, and even though the kids were nice, she wasn't included in any activities. When they rushed out of school together to get a Coke or to go to each other's houses, she wanted to shout, "Wait for me!"

She kicked at a mound of snow, wondering if she'd always be this lonely and miserable. Rows of big Victorian houses, neatly painted with what the original colors must have been, stared cheerily back at her. One three-story house was painted a deep red with gingerbread woodwork trimmed a bright gold. Another house was gray and red with a blue porch, and the one next to hers was green, orange, and turquoise. When Amanda saw Jessica O'Connor, she caught her breath. Jessica was running up the walk and into the large white house on the corner. To think she lived only a few houses from her. Well, Amanda thought, what difference did it make? It might as well be a few miles! Jessica didn't have any time for her. Suddenly a bicycle horn beeped, and she leaped to one side. She recognized the back of Tommy Hach's head. He sat in front of her in English, so she held up her hand and called feebly, "Hi, Tommy." But he didn't answer. Just continued to pedal faster. Maybe he didn't hear her. Or more than likely he didn't even know who she was! No one did!

With a sinking feeling, Amanda turned up the shoveled walk to their gray and white house with its bright red roof covered by patches of snow. It wasn't much fun coming home to an empty house, despite its friendly appearance. Her mother had already started her teaching job at Tinley Junior High. When a math teacher had resigned in the middle of the year, her mother was able to step right in. Her father was downtown at his new job as a staff photographer for the Chicago *Tribune*, and even Philip, her older brother, was gone.

It didn't take Philip long to fit in at Evanston Township High School, she thought with a twinge of envy. His new friend, Ian, had come over the night before to help unpack Philip's magic stuff. Today, after school, Ian was introducing Philip to "The Magic Circle," a group of amateur magicians. Maybe if she were a wonderful magician like Philip she'd make new friends quickly, too. That's what she needed, something to catch the other kids' attention so they'd notice her. She could do a few magic tricks, but not like Philip. He was a master! Maybe if she practiced more. . . .

Unhappily Amanda unlocked the door and went inside. Hanging up her jacket, she picked up the mail, and went into the kitchen for a glass of milk and some cake. Being lonely hadn't taken her appetite away.

Sam, her orange long-haired cat, stretched out his forepaws on the tiled floor and looked up at her expectantly. He opened his pink mouth wide and his "meow" was impatient.

"Hi, Sam," Amanda said. "Are you hungry, too?" She poured a little milk in his saucer, watching him crouch over the dish and daintily lap up the milk. She adored Sam. Four years before, he'd been a scrawny stray that had scratched on their door one bitter cold night. They'd taken him in and her mother had let her keep him for good. The next day the vet estimated that Sam was between two and four years old. She stroked Sam's shiny sleek coat, thinking how well he'd responded to their love and care.

Eating her snack, Amanda gazed out the window at the large oak towering over their backyard and wondered what Jessica O'Connor was doing. It would be nice to have someone to talk to. But Jessica was no doubt on the phone, already talking

13

to one of her many girlfriends. Aimlessly Amanda shuffled through the mail but jerked upright when she noticed a letter addressed to her. She grabbed the envelope and ripped it open. Good old Ann! At least *she* hadn't forgotten her! Quickly Amanda scanned the contents:

January 9

Dear Amanda,

It's lonesome in Mason without you. I've only seen the people that moved into your old house once. They're older and don't have any kids. Every time I go by I look for your blue bike. It's not the same.

The kids at school miss you, too. Even Jennie Olsen asked for your address. I have a feeling you'll be getting a long letter soon with everyone scribbling a line.

George Marek got that shaggy hair of his practically shaved off. He looks almost as goofy as Norman now. Speaking of Norman, he's just as mean as ever. Remember the rocks he kept on his front porch to throw at us? Well, he's still up to his old tricks. Today he almost hit me with a stone, then chased me halfway home! He's such a geek! In science yesterday Heather dropped a test tube of sulfur, and the smell was so rotten that Mr. James opened all the windows. We almost died of frostbite! But I'd rather freeze to death than die of stinky fumes!

I can't think of anything else to write. How do you like your new school? Knowing you, I'll bet you've made a lot of friends, but don't forget your old ones! Like me!

> *Write soon, soon, soon!*
> *Love,*
> *Ann*

Ha! Amanda thought bitterly. Little chance of any new friends here! She reread Ann's letter, remembering the fun they used to have together. Yes, even dodging ugly Norman's stones! Once Ms. Turnbull, the fifth grade teacher, had been furious at Norman for throwing spitballs. She ordered him out in the hall, but Norman wouldn't budge. The more Ms. Turnbull screamed at him the more he clenched his jaw and sat in his desk. Finally Ms. Turnbull pulled his desk out the door, Norman dragging his feet all the way.

Amanda smiled as she folded up Ann's letter.

She'd write to her again tonight. They'd had so many good times together. Like every Halloween. When they were five they dressed up as goblins and knocked on everyone's door in the neighborhood, then ran like crazy. They'd been afraid to knock on the Fyfields' door, because the old couple were always yelling at them to stay off the grass or to quit making so much noise. But that night, she and Ann had been brave and crept up to the door, rapping furiously. They dashed away, but Mr. Fyfield was too fast for them. When Amanda felt his hand on her arm, her heart beat so hard she thought it would jump through her skin. He took them into the house, and Ann clutched Amanda's hand in fright. Seeing Mrs. Fyfield scared her even more. She felt like Gretel facing the wicked witch and wondered if Mrs. Fyfield was about to push them into the oven! Were they surprised when Mr. and Mrs. Fyfield gave them candy and cookies and were really nice!

Then there was the Halloween when she'd been running with Ann in the dark and had slammed into a wire slanting down from a telephone pole. Amanda'd gotten a bad cut above her eye, but it'd been worth it when she got to wear an eye patch to school for two weeks. The year before's Halloween was different and the best one of all. She and Ann gave a Halloween party and invited boys!

They'd bobbed for apples, had a ghost room set up, and told scary stories.

Next Halloween, she thought sadly, she'd be without Ann. Without anyone! Sam rubbed against her pant leg, and she reached down, picked up the big cat, and hugged him. His long whiskers tickled her cheek. No, she wasn't quite alone, she thought, burying her face in Sam's fur and feeling a tear trickle down her nose.

3

Monday morning, seated on the bus, Amanda overheard Jessica and Megan Rollins talking.

"I tell you, Soft Shine is the best shampoo I've ever used," Jessica said, moving her head to and fro and letting her hair swish from side to side. "Just feel it, Megan," she coaxed.

Megan, a girl in Ms. Novak's class who was always with Jessica, took a strand of Jessica's hair between her fingers. "Your hair is like silk," she exclaimed.

Like a sheet of golden satin, thought Amanda, admiring Jessica's beauty from across the aisle.

"Well, I know one thing for sure," Megan said emphatically. "Mother and I are going shopping at Old Orchard after school, and I'm buying some. What is it? Soft . . . ?"

"Soft Shine," replied Jessica, laughing and displaying even, white teeth set against her smooth, glowing skin.

Soft Shine, Amanda repeated to herself. She'd buy some, too. But with her tight curls what good would it do? On the other hand, it might be just the thing to tame her wild hair. After all, it was time she paid more attention to her appearance. These were big-city girls who knew everything about shampoos, makeup, and clothes. She'd never given much thought to shampoo before, but maybe that was her problem. It was time she changed. Glancing sideways at Jessica and Megan, she analyzed what they were wearing. Jessica had on a long navy coat, unbuttoned, and underneath she wore a red plaid shirt with a navy sweater and navy stockings. Her friend, Megan, made a good contrast to Jessica's blonde good looks. She was dark-haired, with a round face. She wore a camel's hair jacket, designer jeans, a rust sweater, and suede high-top shoes. Very chic!

Amanda stared down at her baggy sweater and faded pants that were a size too big. In Iowa when she went horseback riding, she hadn't worn them for style; she'd worn them for comfort. Soberly she gazed out the window at the shopping center near Kennedy. The drugstore might carry Soft Shine. Today after school she'd buy a bottle, plus some bubble bath, and some good soap for her skin. She'd make herself over, that's what she'd do. She'd become beautiful. Then the kids would have to notice her! She'd even let her mother buy

19

her a new outfit. She had been nagging Amanda to get some new clothes, but Amanda hadn't really cared about them until now! Things were going to be different, she thought, lifting her chin, and stepping off the bus.

Jessica and Megan brushed by her, and Jessica said cheerfully, "Hi, Amanda. See you in class."

Amanda gave her a quick smile, but she doubted if Jessica even saw it, for she was already talking and laughing with Megan.

First period! Ugh, she thought, slowing down. To think she had once loved history. Now she dreaded it. Ms. Novak hadn't called on her all week — hadn't even looked in her direction. No doubt she was still miffed at Amanda for blurting out the correct date of Columbus's death in front of the whole class.

Going into the classroom, Amanda almost bumped into Jonathan, who was studying the map. He glanced at her and his grin lit up his whole face. "Hi," he said. "How do you like Kennedy?"

"It's okay," she said evenly, not wanting him to know how much she missed Jefferson School in Mason. She managed a smile and was about to ask him if he was a swimmer when Ms. Novak said sternly, "That's the first bell. Everyone sit down."

Her one opportunity to talk to Jonathan, and

Ms. Novak had to tell them to sit down! Well, she'd ask him just one question, anyway. "Jonathan," she asked, "are you on the swim team?"

But before he could reply, Ms. Novak snapped, "Amanda, that means you!"

Without another word, Amanda sat down. Today she had a plan that might make Ms. Novak call on her, and she didn't want to ruin it by making her any more angry than she already was. Amanda was tired of being ignored.

After Ms. Novak reminded them that their essays on the New World explorers were due the next day, she asked questions about their last reading assignment. "How were Spanish colonies unlike the English settlements?" Amanda waved her hand, but Ms. Novak looked beyond her and nodded at William.

"Who were the Sea Dogs and what was their purpose?" Again Ms. Novak looked away from Amanda and called on Megan.

After being passed over for four more questions, on the fifth one Amanda raised a placard on a stick and jiggled it up and down. Printed on the cardboard were the words:

PLEASE CALL ON ME. I KNOW THE ANSWER.

For a moment all Ms. Novak could do was stare. She lifted her eyebrows, and her mouth formed a big O. All at once Jessica giggled. Soon the whole class burst out laughing. Amanda shot Ms. Novak a worried look but was delighted when her teacher's mouth turned up at the corners. "All right, Amanda," Ms. Novak said with a chuckle. "Why were the French in the New World different than the Spanish and English?"

Amanda answered the question easily, explaining that the French were more interested in furs than settling the land.

Ms. Novak nodded approvingly. "Very good, Amanda," she said, and the tension between them seemed to evaporate. At least Amanda hoped so.

Jonathan, who sat in the row across from her, nodded and gave her a thumbs-up.

On the way to science, Jessica caught up with her. "You sure do know your history," she said in admiration.

Amanda laughed. "I read a lot of history. My dad has a big collection of books on American history. I guess I just take after him." She glanced at Jessica, happy to talk to her. "Do you have your essay finished for tomorrow?" she asked, not wanting their conversation to end.

"Yes, it's ready to hand in."

"Oh," Amanda said, her voice dropping in disappointment. She wanted to ask Jessica to come over so they could work on their writing together.

"There's Laura," Jessica said, dashing ahead. "See you in science, Amanda."

So far the day had gone well. The history class had seemed friendly and had laughed at the placard. It made her feel good. Even Ms. Novak had smiled.

But on Friday her good feelings disappeared. When Ms. Novak returned their essays, Amanda couldn't believe the big red D at the top of her paper. A D she thought, her stomach twisting into one big knot. She'd never gotten a D in her life, let alone in history. Ms. Novak *did* hate her! There was no doubt about it! For a long time Amanda stared at her paper. When Ms. Novak gave them study time, Amanda agonized over what she should do. Should she ask why she'd gotten such a low grade? She noticed several kids went up to talk to the teacher. Should she? What good would it do?

Amanda watched Ms. Novak, whose back was turned to her as she wrote on the board. Finally, stiffening her spine, Amanda went up to see what she'd done wrong.

"M-Ms. Novak?" she said between trembling lips. "I — I wanted to ask you about my grade. . . ."

Ms. Novak stopped writing, the chalk held daintily between her fingers. "What you wrote,

Amanda, was excellent," she said, tilting her head sympathetically, "but you misread the question. Look, let me show you," she said, turning to her desk.

Amanda pushed the swivel chair aside so she could stand next to Ms. Novak. How could she have misread the question? she puzzled. But if she had, that would explain her low grade.

All at once Ms. Novak went to sit down but her chair wasn't there. Astonished, Amanda watched as Ms. Novak frantically clutched at her desk, spilling papers, paper clips, rubber bands, pencils, books, and a box of staples.

Amanda lurched to catch Ms. Novak, but only succeeded in grabbing her long string of beads. Horrified, Amanda stared first at Ms. Novak sprawled on the floor, then at the one blue bead nestled in her hand. The rest were rolling and bouncing all over the room.

"Oh, no," Amanda groaned. What a klutz! She bent down to help Ms. Novak, but the young teacher was too quick for her, and when she jumped up, the two of them banged heads. "Ouch," Amanda said, rubbing her temple and sinking to the floor.

She held her head in her hands, not daring to look at Ms. Novak. Now she'd really blown it. She couldn't remember when she'd felt so awful.

"Are you all right, Amanda?" Ms. Novak asked.

Amanda kept her head down, her cheeks burning. "I — I think so," she said, too embarrassed to look at the class.

"Here," Ms. Novak said. Amanda glanced up and saw Ms. Novak's outstretched hand. "Let me help you."

Amanda gulped. This was the worst thing that had ever happened to her. But Ms. Novak didn't seem mad, which made her feel all the worse. How could she have done such a dumb, terrible thing? Oh, floor, she wished, open up and swallow me whole. Shakily she took Ms. Novak's hand and stood up. She dared to glance at the class and was surprised that everyone wore a big smile, not wanting to laugh out loud at Ms. Novak. But since the teacher was taking it so well, one by one they burst into giggles.

"Help me pick up my beads, Amanda," Ms. Novak said briskly, her eyes twinkling.

Embarrassed, Amanda crawled beneath the desk, gathering one blue bead after another. There must be thousands, she thought in despair. Despite Ms. Novak's smile, she knew it was just a show. She really must be furious at her!

4

But the next week began calmly for Amanda and Ms. Novak didn't seem upset. And the change in Jessica was great. She was much more friendly on the way to science. Every time she mentioned Ms. Novak's spill her tinkling laugh rang pleasantly in Amanda's ears.

On Monday Amanda got to class early, and Jonathan was already studying the globe. "Hey," he asked with a grin, giving the world a spin, "when are you and Ms. Novak going to crawl around after more beads?"

"Never!" she stated emphatically.

Most of the kids brushed past them now, chattering and jostling one another, but Amanda didn't notice. She could only look at Jonathan.

"Know any more funny tricks?" Jonathan teased, his brown eyes as dark and soft as his hair.

"Oh, one or two," she said, trying to seem casual.

"You do?" Jonathan said, backing away from her. "You're not going to pull my chair out from under me, are you?"

Amanda smiled. "Nooo," she said lightly. "Something much better than that." She remembered the tricks Philip had taught her, and her fingers were itching to perform some magic. "Just stand still, Jonathan." She tilted her head to one side. "I see something shiny behind your ear." Reaching behind his head, she brought forth a nickel, twirling it around. Holding it, she waved her left hand over the coin and said, "Abracadabra," and the nickel disappeared.

"How'd you do that?" he asked, staring at Amanda's empty hands. "Where'd you learn that?"

"Oh, here and there," she answered mysteriously. "But don't you know a magician never gives away any tricks?"

All at once Ms. Novak closed the classroom door, and walked to the front of the room. "Everyone please sit down," she said briskly. "Take out pen and paper for your history test."

"That's a neat trick, Amanda," Jonathan said, taking his seat across from her. "Know any more?"

"Oh, a few," she murmured with a secret smile, relishing his admiring look.

"Do it again," he coaxed.

"Later," she whispered, noticing Ms. Novak's frown.

27

The next day, though, she not only did the coin trick but also pulled a whole string of scarves from Jonathan's shirt front.

"Oh, Amanda, do the scarf trick for me," Jessica begged.

Amanda laughed gleefully. "I have something better in mind for you, Jessica."

Jessica clapped her hands. "What is it? Show me."

"Be seated, Amanda, and put away the scarves," Ms. Novak warned.

But Amanda had already begun to pull out several silk roses from Jessica's sleeve. Even if she wanted to, she wouldn't be able to stop. She was enjoying the laughter of the class, Jessica's astonishment, and Jonathan's admiration too much.

"Amanda!" Ms. Novak said sharply. "Sit down!"

Amanda hastily gathered up the roses and slipped into her desk.

Jessica glanced at her and smiled.

Amanda felt a warm glow. She'd been here for weeks, and this was the first time she felt noticed and liked. It seemed so obvious all she had to do to have friends was to be funny.

On the way to science, Jessica even invited her to come over after school and have a Coke. Megan and Heather, her two best friends, would be there, too.

* * *

Sitting in the O'Connors' big sunny kitchen, laughing with Jessica and her friends, made Amanda feel part of a group for the first time. A month was a long time to wait to be included, and she was eager to write and tell Ann tonight. From the time she'd arrived in Evanston her letters had been filled with gloom and doom. She knew Ann would be glad for some cheery news.

"That was so funny when you pulled the roses out of Jessica's sleeve," Megan said, her plump face breaking into a smile.

"Ms. Novak wasn't amused, though," Heather said, jiggling the ice in her glass.

"No, Kathy Novak wasn't laughing, was she?" Jessica said. "She's a darling, but she needs to lighten up."

"Maybe she has her mind on other things," Heather said. "I hear she's going to be married as soon as school's out."

"How old do you think she is?" Megan questioned.

Jessica shrugged. "Probably in her twenties."

"I thought she was a student when I first came into her classroom," Amanda said. "She's so tiny."

"Cute figure, too. Wonder what she does for fun," Heather said.

"If she's going to be married, she probably sees her boyfriend a lot."

"Well, I know one thing," Amanda said. "She doesn't like me."

"You're too much of a cut-up," Megan said, shaking her head. "The way you make things disappear is amazing." She grinned, touching the metal fastenings on her teeth that glittered in the sunlight. "I wish you could make my braces disappear."

Amanda grinned. "I wish I could, too, but," she said, hunching up her shoulders in mock despair, "I'm just a poor magician who only knows a few tricks."

"Who taught you?" Jessica asked, popping open another can and refilling glasses all around.

"My brother Philip."

"Oh, I've seen him go into your house. He's a hunk! Serious-looking, though," Jessica said.

It was the first time Amanda had heard Philip described as a "hunk," but she supposed to an outsider, he was. She couldn't see it, for even though he was tall and broad-shouldered, his square face was overshadowed by a crooked nose. "He can be a pain, though," Amanda admitted. "He's always teasing me about my frizzy hair." She held out a hank of her wiry red coils.

Jessica smoothed back her long golden hair. "You know, I'll bet we could tame your mane." She smiled, her blue eyes twinkling.

"You could?" Amanda asked in wonder. "Now

30

that'd be a magic trick I'd love to learn."

Heather laughed. "Jessica knows all about beauty tricks." Her dark eyes narrowed as she studied Amanda's hair. "What would you do, Jess? Use Soft Shine shampoo and then the mousse?"

Jessica's head bobbed up and down. "Yup. It worked for Megan, and I know it will work on Amanda."

"Right," Megan said. "I used to use a can of mousse a week, but since I cut my hair I only use half a can."

Amanda joined in with their laughter, noticing Megan's short dark hair that framed her globe-shaped face. But on that globe was a very friendly map, thought Amanda, settling back in her chair, and enjoying Jessica's friends.

With a sudden thought, Jessica snapped her fingers. "How about everyone coming over Saturday night, and we'll shampoo and mousse Amanda's hair? Then we'll rent a movie and pop popcorn."

"Terrific," Megan said enthusiastically.

"Cool," echoed Heather. "What time?"

"About seven, OK?" She glanced at Amanda.

"Sure," agreed Amanda, knowing her mom and dad would be delighted. They didn't have to worry about Philip, who had fit right in with the ninth grade. With his winning personality and magic tricks, Philip always made friends easily. But she could tell her mother was concerned about her by the way she'd been urging her to invite someone to the house. But how could she have friends over when she didn't have any?

Now, though, things would be different, Amanda thought happily as she sat in Jessica's kitchen, basking in the warmth of her new friends. Amanda smiled. She and the kids at Kennedy were going to get along just fine!

5

At supper that night Amanda spooned up the last of her apple cobbler. "May I go over to Jessica O'Connor's Saturday night?" she enquired, trying to keep the lilt out of her voice.

Sarah Kingsley's clear hazel eyes focused warmly on her daughter. "Why, Amanda, when did this come about? I didn't know you were friends with Jessica."

"Oh, yes," Amanda said casually. "Megan and Heather and I went over to Jessica's after school today, and we're going to rent a movie and pop corn Saturday. If," she said, glancing first at her father, then at her mother, "I can go." She certainly didn't intend to tell them about the shampoo and mousse. Her hair was too hopeless to expect any miracles.

Paul Kingsley pushed back his chair and rose to his full six feet. He was getting a paunch, and jogged like fury every morning to get rid of it. Sometimes Amanda thought his favorite activities were eating and then running off the calories. "The O'Connors live on the corner, don't they?" he asked, shoving his horn-rimmed glasses up on his high-bridged nose.

"Three doors away," Amanda said. Sam rubbed against her legs, and she reached down and scratched one ear.

"I don't see any reason why Amanda can't go, do you Sarah?" He gave his wife a quizzical look.

Sarah nodded happily. "As long as you're home by ten, Amanda."

"Oh, I will be," Amanda agreed, only too eager to promise any time if she could only go.

Philip reached over and pinched Amanda's cheek. "Little sister's met a friend at last." He chuckled.

Amanda sometimes wanted to punch Philip's craggy nose. Four years before he'd been in a fight and broken his nose, leaving a hump right in the middle. He reminded her of Dick Tracy. What's more she'd like to give him a second crook in his nose to match the first one when he acted so superior!

"Temper, temper," he teased. "Your red hair is frizzing up!" He burst out laughing.

"Just because you met Ian the first day," she sputtered, "you think you're the only one with a friend!"

"Okay, you two. Clear the table," Sarah Kingsley ordered, but she smiled at Amanda as if the two shared a secret.

Amanda smiled back. She was too happy to really mind Philip's remark. In fact, because she had a favor to ask of her brother, she'd better keep on his good side.

When she and Philip were putting the dishes in the dishwasher, she asked, "Philip, will you teach me an easy trick that I can do tomorrow?"

"That's tricky," he joked. "But I'll give it a try. Have you done the scarf trick I taught you?"

"Yes, and it worked. The kids really thought it was neat."

"Then I guess you're ready for some new magic. I'll show you the gum trick, but Ian's coming at eight so we don't have much time."

After the dishes were finished and the countertops shined, Philip pulled a pack of gum from his pocket. He extracted one stick and tucked it into his left hand. "I'll bet you can't guess which hand the stick of gum is in!"

Amanda looked at him warily. "But I've got a fifty-fifty chance."

Philip's green eyes, a pale imitation of her own, danced with merriment. "I'll bet you'll miss every time," he predicted.

"Try me," she said cautiously, knowing Philip's long, deft fingers could move as fast as lightning. He was clever, working his magic with one hand

35

while he did mysterious things with the other. He realized a person couldn't watch two things at once.

Philip held out his two closed fists in front of him. "Which hand has the gum?" he questioned.

She grinned at him, tapping his left hand.

"Wrong," he chortled. "It's here," and opened his right hand, which held the stick of gum.

Four more times he tried the trick, and four more times she chose the wrong hand. "I give up," she said finally. "How did you do it?"

"Easy. Before you begin, have a stick of gum slipped into the back of your belt. When you put your hands behind your back take the second stick of gum in your other hand. Now both hands have sticks of gum, so no matter which hand they choose, you can win. If they choose the left, open your right and say, 'Wrong, it's over here.' "

She nodded. It was an easy trick, yet it would be puzzling. It would fool Jonathan, she was sure.

"Here's your reward for being a good sport, Amanda," Philip said with a chuckle, handing her a stick of gum.

She took the gum and thought what fun it'd be to try the trick on Jonathan the next day.

"Don't give them time to tell you to open *both* hands," Philip said, wagging a finger under her nose. "Immediately put them behind your back again." He paused. "Otherwise you'll wind up with egg on your face!"

She giggled. "Better egg than gum!"

Just then the doorbell rang. "There's Ian. Be a good little girl and go do your homework."

She rolled her eyes in exasperation, wishing he wouldn't treat her like a younger sister!

The next day Amanda came to school early, and just as she thought, Jonathan was there working on his outline map.

"What'cha doing?" she asked, bubbling inside.

"Putting in dotted lines to show Vasco da Gama's voyage." He glanced up at her and grinned. "Why?"

"Oh, I thought you might have time to see a new trick."

He leaned back in his desk, folding his arms. "Great. Show me."

Carefully she opened a fresh pack of gum before him, then proceeded to fool him. Every time he guessed which hand the stick of gum was in, he was wrong.

"Hey, how'd you . . . ?" His voice trailed off, and he grinned sheepishly. "I know. You don't need to tell me. A magician never gives away her tricks."

"Right," she answered him, offering him a stick

of gum. Was it only the month before she'd felt like an awkward newcomer? Now she had friends! What a difference it made to have someone to laugh with. That empty feeling inside had completely disappeared.

When Megan and Jessica came in, she gave them each a stick of gum, too.

"Amanda!" Ms. Novak's voice crackled throughout the room. "I wish you wouldn't hand out gum in my classroom. Put it away at once!"

Amanda groaned silently. Of all the times for Ms. Novak to come into the room. Just once she wished she could be doing something that Ms. Novak would praise her for! And to think that the last few days things had been fairly smooth between them. But it didn't take her long to botch things up!

"Put the gum away," Ms. Novak repeated.

Hastily Amanda stuffed the gum into her pocket. "Sorry," she muttered, taking her seat.

Ms. Novak, looking chic in a brown-checkered pants suit and creamy satin blouse, asked for everyone's attention. "Today," she said with a smile, "everyone will pick a slip of paper with the name of someone we've studied this year." She held up a shoe box stuffed with paper that had been sitting on her desk. "You'll have three minutes to try to show us who your character is.

Use any props you want to, but you can give only one oral clue. You may also borrow anything you need from a classmate or from me." She proceeded to go down the aisles, letting everyone pick a slip, then perched on the edge of her desk and dangled her feet. Her short, thick hair fell naturally into rich waves, and her eyes sparkled with pleasure as she surveyed her students. Amanda hated to admit it, but Ms. Novak was very pretty.

Everyone immediately set to work, making signs or getting props for their character. Jonathan asked Ms. Novak if he could use the yardstick while Jessica borrowed her scarf. Amanda wondered what character Jonathan had drawn. As for herself, she was delighted with her historical figure. Queen Elizabeth! And she knew exactly how she'd portray the English monarch. First she cut out a paper crown; then she borrowed Megan's gold chain, Heather's silver necklace, and Jessica's opal ring.

"Be careful of that ring," Jessica warned. "It was my grandmother's."

"I will," Amanda promised, looking about. She needed more jewelry. Queen Elizabeth was famous for her rich gowns and fabulous jewels! Did she dare ask to borrow Ms. Novak's newly restrung blue beads? Yes, she would, she thought determinedly. Everyone else was borrowing things from Ms. Novak.

When Jonathan was called on, he acted out a feeble, bent-over old man who limped about with a cane, searching for something. When he discovered a glass of water on Ms. Novak's desk, his eyes grew round with astonishment. Eagerly he sprinkled a few drops over his head. When the drops took effect, he all at once jerked upright and flung away his yardstick. He began to romp around the room like a two-year-old.

Immediately Amanda held up her hand. "I know. I know," she cried gleefully. It was Ponce de León, the Spanish explorer who had searched for the Fountain of Youth in Florida. When Jonathan nodded in her direction, she gave the right answer. Since she was correct, she was next.

Regally Amanda stepped to the front of the room, and when she slowly turned to face the class, she kicked at an imaginary dress train trailing behind her. With her nose in the air, she gazed haughtily about the room, fingering her three necklaces. She remembered Ms. Novak hadn't been too keen on lending her the long blue beads, so she handled them gingerly between two fingers. But she was pleased with the desired effect they created. Along with her paper crown and high paper collar, she not only had the appearance of a queen, but felt like one, too. She cleared her throat and recited:

" 'Ride a cock horse to Banbury Cross
To see a fine lady on a white horse,
With rings on her fingers and bells on her toes
She shall have music wherever she goes.' "

Jessica waved her hand frantically. Amanda, smiling, called on her.

"Queen Elizabeth," Jessica promptly said.

Ms. Novak was pleased. "The nursery rhyme about Elizabeth was a good touch, Amanda."

Amanda glowed at her teacher's praise. She walked over to hand Ms. Novak the blue beads but was horrified when they slithered down into her hands without her so much as touching them. The clasp had broken. Her heart fluttered wildly. Not again. She hadn't even laid a hand on the beads. She and the blue beads must be jinxed. That was all there was to it.

"Th-the clasp must have broken," Amanda said weakly, holding up the blue strand like a dead snake.

The class broke into laughter and Amanda stood with her shoulders hunched, utterly deflated. In one minute's time she'd gone from being a queen to a fool! It could happen only to her. Uneasily she glanced at Ms. Novak, who carefully took the beads from Amanda.

"Don't worry, Amanda," she said quickly. "It was an accident."

But Amanda noticed that even though Ms. Novak's lips were stretched into a smile, her eyes were icy-blue.

6

Friday, before first period, Amanda went directly to her locker. Opening the red metal door, she thought with surprise how much she was beginning to like Kennedy, which was a very unusual and attractive school. She liked the way the first floor lockers were painted a bright red, the second floor's an emerald-green, and the third floor's a brilliant turquoise. Her counselor, Ms. Loomis, was nice, too, and so were all her teachers except for Ms. Novak. On Thursday things had really unraveled between them. The least little thing she did put Ms. Novak in a tizzy.

Pulling her history notebook from her locker shelf, she wished she could throw it in the trash, instead. She could be sitting just minding her own business, when Ms. Novak would snap at her for no reason at all. Of course, she thought she had to shoulder some of the blame. She must really be a pest. But a lot of her antics hadn't been done on purpose. She supposed she should stop her magic tricks, but they were too much of a hit. It seemed the more she performed, the more the kids liked her. And, she thought, the more Ms. Novak hated her. Couldn't Ms. Novak enjoy her magic, too? Did she have to be such a sourpuss? Where was her sense of humor?

Amanda blew away a wisp of hair that had fallen across her forehead, and wondered why Ms. Novak disliked her so much. It couldn't just be the beads she'd broken and her magic.

Couldn't Ms. Novak understand that when the kids laughingly urged Amanda to do just one more piece of magic, she just couldn't stop? Even without her magic she could make them laugh. Breaking the blue beads had been horrible, but when the class laughed, she found the experience hadn't been all bad. And what could be more important than their laughter ringing in her ears? Funny, Ms. Novak's class was the only one in which she got into so many scrapes. Yet it was in history where she'd made all her friends, too. Amanda thought that being liked was worth facing Ms. Novak's anger.

She hadn't heard the lockers bang or the shouts until Jessica stopped in front of her. "Amanda, aren't you going to class?"

"I'd like to stay away from history as long as possible," she grumbled, trudging wearily alongside Jessica. Once again she'd have to confront Ms. Novak. She still had months to deal with her! Could she stand it?

"Ms. Novak really is on your case," Jessica said. "I'll never forget the look on her face yesterday when you opened your hand and out popped a bunch of paper flowers." She giggled. "Her face turned so red I thought she was going to burst."

"Ummmhmmm," Amanda agreed. All at once she had a funny feeling in the pit of her stomach, knowing that Ms. Novak must be at her wit's end.

"Hi," Jonathan said, easily falling in with them.

"Wait a sec," Jessica said, pausing before her locker. "I need to pick up my science notebook."

"What's new?" Jonathan asked, leaning his thin frame against a locker.

"Nothing new, Jonathan," Jessica replied, quickly twirling her locker combination. "Except Amanda and Ms. Novak aren't getting along."

Jonathan grinned. "That's new?" He faced Amanda. "You're funny, Amanda. Since you entered Kennedy, history's become fun. Every day you do something different. I don't know where you learn everything."

She returned his smile, not saying anything. Little did he know how she had to wheedle and beg Philip into teaching her a new piece of magic almost every night. She even bribed him by doing the dishes all by herself. And Jonathan's words, "Every day you do something different," nagged at her. How could she keep it up?

Amanda sat through history, determined not to do or say anything to annoy Ms. Novak. Her teacher looked pretty today in a sapphire-blue sweater that set off her clear eyes, eyes that were fringed by long dark lashes. Once when Ms. Novak asked questions about the reading, she called on Amanda, giving her a wary look. Politely Amanda answered the question. Ms. Novak, she thought silently, I'm a nice girl. Give me a break, and I know you'll like me. See how well I can behave? She folded her hands in front of her and stared straight ahead, not hearing Ms. Novak.

"Amanda!" Ms. Novak rapped out sharply. "Didn't you hear me? I'll repeat what I just said: Take out paper and pencil for a pop quiz."

She felt her cheeks turn pink as she hurriedly ripped out a page from her notebook. To top it all off, she hadn't read the night's assignment, either. She'd been too busy learning another of Philip's tricks. But she was confident she'd know the answers. She'd studied most of this history before. She'd be able to ace this test, she was sure of it.

Ms. Novak handed out the quiz, and Amanda found it wasn't as easy as she thought. It was on the *Mayflower* and the settlement of Jamestown, and she racked her brain for facts about the signing of the Mayflower Compact or the way James-town was governed. Nuts, she thought glumly. Everything was going down the drain!

Suddenly in the midst of the quiet, except for scratching pencils, a bee lit on her paper. Her mouth dropped open, and she reared back, gasping. The yellow-and-black-striped bee seemed groggy, but when she swatted at it with her notebook and missed, it came angrily alive. In a fury it buzzed and darted about her head. "Ooooh," Amanda squealed, ducking and dodging. She finally shooed away the bee, only to have it latch onto her sleeve. "Oooh, no," she panted, frantically flapping her arm.

"Amanda! Be quiet!" Ms. Novak hissed. "We're taking a test!"

But she couldn't be quiet. The bee had crawled up her sleeve. She yelled, leaping up and dancing a little jig. "A bee! A bee!" she screamed, wildly shaking her arms and continuing to stomp about crazily.

The bee dropped on the floor, crawling under her desk. Backing away, Amanda pointed wide-eyed at the floor, too scared to utter a word.

"What on earth has gotten into you, Amanda?" Ms. Novak asked impatiently, standing up and peering at Amanda's desk.

At last Amanda recovered her voice. "A bee crawled up my arm," she whispered.

47

"A bee?" Ms. Novak repeated, her eyebrows shooting up in surprise. "In February?"

"Yes," Amanda retorted positively. She had no idea why a bee had come to torment her in February rather than in May. Maybe it had been hibernating somewhere or escaped from the zoo or had flown in from Hawaii. How should she know?

"Where is the bee?" her teacher asked in a chilly tone as she shook her head in exasperation.

"On the floor!" Amanda said urgently. "On the floor, under my desk!"

The class was in an uproar. Several kids jumped up. Others ran for the door.

"Everyone *sit down*! I don't see any bee," Ms. Novak said, trying to reassure everyone. She glared at Amanda.

Jonathan bravely searched around Amanda's desk but turned to Ms. Novak and shrugged his shoulders. "I don't see anything," he said. He glanced back at Amanda with a funny smile.

Indignantly she stared back. Did he think she was making this up?

"There's no bee, Amanda," Ms. Novak snapped, and a dark warning cloud had settled over her features. "Sit down and finish your quiz."

"It's — it's under my desk," she stammered. "It dropped off of my sleeve. . . ."

"Yes, yes, and just like magic you made it disappear," Ms. Novak observed sarcastically. "Sit down," she repeated, folding her arms across her chest, "and finish your quiz. Let's have no more of your demonstrations."

Amanda knew she meant business, so she gingerly sat down. "But there was a bee," she said lamely, peeking under her desk. The class laughed, no doubt thinking she was just being silly again. The bee had to be somewhere near, she thought, cautiously lifting her left foot. Then a terrifying new idea hit her. What if it had crept up her jeans?

Shuffling her feet and searching all around, she couldn't concentrate. She didn't care if she failed the stupid quiz. The fat bee was the only thing on her mind. Maybe it had hidden in the floor crack along the wall. Or maybe it was on her leg ready to sting.

Suddenly the bee reappeared, crawling up on a blackboard eraser. Amanda jumped up, pointing at the chalkboard. "There's the bee!" she shrieked.

"Amanda Kingsley!" Ms. Novak said grimly. "Sit down!"

Jonathan craned his neck and rolled up his notebook, ready to attack. "I see it," he said gleefully, moving stealthily toward the blackboard.

Just then the bee spread its wings and circled

the room. The kids, screaming and yelling, ducked and bumped into one another in their haste to get out of its way.

Stunned, Ms. Novak, her eyes growing big, stared in disbelief. "Class," she said weakly. "Sit down." But either she wasn't heard or no one paid any attention. Then, when the bee buzzed around Ms. Novak's head, she picked up a sheaf of papers and began to beat the air wildly.

Amanda forgot her fear and tried to shoo the bee away from Ms. Novak by using her notebook to hit it. She struck a vicious blow but hit Ms. Novak's arm instead.

"Ouch!" Ms. Novak exclaimed, backing away from Amanda and clutching her upper arm. "*You're* a—a—menace," she sputtered. All at once the bee dived at them, and she and Amanda became one big tangle of four flopping arms attached to two weaving and dodging bodies.

"Amanda," Ms. Novak gasped, "get away from me!"

The bee hovered over Ms. Novak's desk, then lit on a book. Jonathan dashed up, hitting at the elusive bee, but it flew off before he could get a good shot. He did manage, however, to scatter papers and books on the floor.

When the bee swooped down on Amanda, she struck out, sending it flying in Ms. Novak's direction. The striped bee landed on her wrist. Mesmerized, Ms. Novak stared at the bee. All at once she flung her papers into the air, letting out a howl of pain. "It stung me!" she wailed.

"Oh, Ms. Novak," Amanda said in dismay, approaching her. "Let me help you." She held out her hands, horrified that Ms. Novak had been stung. Somehow she knew she'd get the blame, even though she couldn't control a bee!

"Don't touch me, Amanda," the teacher warned, rubbing her wrist.

Now the bee flew to the blackboard where Jonathan swatted it.

Speechless, Ms. Novak glanced about her classroom. Papers were scattered everywhere. Students were at the window, by the door, at the blackboard, and some stood on their desktops while others hid under their desks.

Finding her voice, Ms. Novak said, in a trembling tone, "Forget the quiz, class. You're dismissed!"

Everyone bolted for the door except for Amanda. "C-can I do anything?" Amanda asked forlornly, looking at the angry red welt that had already risen on Ms. Novak's wrist.

"No, Amanda, you've done enough for one day," she answered in a choked voice. "Besides, it's only a bee sting. I'll get some ointment from the nurse." She gave Amanda an exasperated look. "If you'd left the bee alone, none of this would have happened."

"But the bee was crawling up my sleeve," Amanda protested indignantly.

"Yes, yes," Ms. Novak said impatiently, "and I don't blame you for what happened. But please," she begged, "just leave!"

Blindly Amanda whirled about and rushed out into the hall. Even when she tried to be helpful, Ms. Novak pushed her away. When the bee had come out of hiding, Ms. Novak could see she hadn't lied. But despite Ms. Novak's words, she knew she'd be blamed for the bee sting, anyway!

"Wow," Jessica said, waiting for Amanda. "There really was a bee! Poor Ms. Novak!"

"I know," Amanda groaned. "How can she stand to look at me after this?"

Jessica giggled. "How can she help it? You're always in the middle of things!"

"Amanda!" Jonathan called, catching up with her. "You sure can shake things up!" His mouth twitched with amusement. "What's next?"

What's next, indeed, she thought, a suffocating sensation tightening her throat. In one short month she'd managed to change a nice normal teacher into a howling banshee and a nice normal classroom into a wild free-for-all!

7

Saturday night at Jessica's house, Amanda forgot all about Ms. Novak and the bee. Instead she was caught up in the new clothes Jessica had bought.

"It was great today," Jessica said, her blue eyes sparkling. "Mom and I shopped at Marshall Field's in Chicago." She opened a box, whipping out a pale peach sweater and a pair of tan cotton pants with big pockets. "Ta da!" she sang out.

"Isn't it darling?" she asked, holding up the delicate pastel sweater against her porcelain skin and golden hair. The top made her look as pretty as a peach sundae, Amanda thought. If I wore that color next to my red hair and freckles, I'd look like a speckled lobster.

"I'm wearing this outfit to Jonathan's party," Jessica announced.

"Jonathan's having a party?" Amanda asked in a bewildered voice, dropping her lashes quickly to hide her hurt.

"Umm-hmm, on St. Patrick's Day," Megan said from her cross-legged position on the tiled kitchen floor. "Hasn't he asked you yet?" She looked up at Amanda with eyes as bright and round as two brown buttons.

"No," Amanda answered, trying to paste a smile on her face. She remembered Jonathan's laughter when he chased after the buzzing bee. And how he'd smiled at her when he told her that she always shook things up. Well, she'd tried to make him laugh, and where did it get her? He didn't even invite her to his party!

"Oh, Jonathan will get around to asking you, Amanda," Heather said offhandedly as she poured a Coke.

"Right," agreed Megan, contentedly munching on an apple. "He only asked us yesterday after school. You'd already left, Amanda."

Yes, she thought gloomily, he invited everyone except me. She hoped her disappointment didn't show. It was embarrassing to find out from her girlfriends, all of whom had been invited. How could Jonathan do this to her? She'd like to tell him what she thought of him. It was because he constantly egged her on that she was always getting into trouble. But she realized it wasn't fair to blame Jonathan. He wasn't the only one who coaxed her to do funny things. Besides, she didn't have to do them. She was the one who went ahead and performed like a trained seal!

"Come on, Amanda," Jessica said, jumping up. "Before we watch the movie we're going to shampoo that mop of yours."

Amanda grinned. "Let's get at it," she said, feeling better when she looked at Heather, Megan, and Jessica. It wasn't long ago she didn't have anyone.

"Lean over the sink," Jessica ordered while she threw a towel around Amanda's slender shoulders. "Hand me the shampoo, will you, Heather?" Jessica said.

Amanda doused her thick hair in the warm water, and Jessica's fingers deftly made soapy swirls in Amanda's wet hair.

After the shampoo, Jessica sprayed Amanda's hair, rinsing out the soap. "Now, we mousse," she said jubilantly.

As if lathering in mousse would make any difference in her springy hair, Amanda thought. But the word "mousse" intrigued her, and the way her three friends hovered around her, she wondered if it really could work miracles.

After Jessica had blown dry her hair, Amanda grinned at the oh's and ah's of the girls. She had to rush to the mirror to see what all the fuss was about. She gasped at the way her rust-red hair curved in a soft line with a few wisps falling on her forehead. The freckles, dotting her cheeks and nose, attractively brought out her jade-green eyes. Even her face didn't seem so thin. She fluffed up her hair, marveling at the way it fell back into place. "I love it!" she exclaimed.

"You look terrific," Jessica said, pushing one of Amanda's curls back.

"I can't believe one can of mousse could make such a change," Amanda said.

"Wait until Jonathan sees you," Heather added.

Jonathan! She hadn't thought about him during this whole transformation, but maybe her new look would get an invitation out of him!

Even her father complimented her on her new hairdo. And Sarah Kingsley gave her daughter a big hug. "You look wonderful, darling," she said, touching Amanda's softer hair.

On Sunday night the O'Connors and Kingsleys got together for bridge, while Amanda and Jessica worked on the history paper that was due the next day. When they took a break, Amanda leaned back, smiling at Jessica. It seemed so natural that they'd become good friends. Was it only six weeks before that she'd envied Jessica her loveliness, her popularity, and her intelligence? She remembered thinking that she'd never get to know her. Now she was her best friend!

* * *

Monday morning, on the way to school, Amanda's boots sloshed through the slushy snow. The sunny day would soon melt the snowdrifts and icicles.

When she came to the stadium, several boys were scuffling in the snow, but up ahead a group of kids, including Jessica and Jonathan, were having a snowball fight.

"Come on, Amanda," Jessica shouted. "We need you! It's the Reds against the Blues and Greens."

Because of her red jacket Amanda was on the side of anyone wearing red. Dropping her notebook and history book, she dashed to Jessica's side. Fortunately they could hide behind the stadium to fling their flying missiles, because there was no snowball throwing on school grounds.

The snow packed into rock-hard balls, and she flung one that caught Jonathan on the side of the head, knocking his ear muffs aslant.

"Wanna play rough, huh?" he yelled, laughing and chasing her beyond the safe stadium walls.

Shrieking, she held up her arms to ward off his pelting snowballs, then with a laugh scooped up a mound of wet snow and flung it at him. Taunting her, Jonathan ran back to his side. She hadn't realized she was unprotected by the stadium walls and was in full view of the school grounds until she heard her name called.

57

For a moment she stood frozen like an ice statue.

"Amanda Kingsley!"

She slowly turned. Oh, no, she moaned to herself, wouldn't Ms. Novak just have to be the teacher on playground duty! And clearly she'd broken the rules! She was a mess, too. Her jacket and pants were covered with snow!

"Amanda!" Ms. Novak said in a disappointed tone. "I'll have to give you three detentions for fighting on the school grounds. Why do you *do* these things?" She shook her head. "I don't want to keep punishing you, Amanda, but you keep breaking the rules. Go inside," she said, her voice softening, "and get dried off."

"May I pick up my books?" Amanda asked.

"Yes, of course," she said, pulling her parka around her head and watching Amanda scamper beyond the walls.

Amanda hurried back to where she'd tossed her books. "Jessica," she called. "Ms. Novak's on duty, and I got nabbed for throwing snowballs. You'd better stop."

Laughing and rosy-cheeked, Jessica ran to her side. "What did Ms. Novak do?"

"I got three detentions." Amanda shrugged her shoulders, as if this was to be expected. "She hates me!"

"Hey! Amanda!" Jonathan shouted, hurrying to

58

join them. "Can you come to my party on Saturday?" He gasped for breath, brushing off his snow-covered jeans.

She nodded. "I'd love to." Then added, "I'll have to ask my parents, but I'm sure it's okay. What time?" she asked, stooping down and picking up her books.

"Seven o'clock. And," he said with a grin, "wear green for St. Patrick's Day." He turned and raced off.

"I will," Amanda called, but her smile quickly faded when she saw the condition of her history book and notebook. She'd carelessly thrown them into a melting snowbank where they'd not only been trampled but soaked through, as well. Both were ruined. With a thumping heart she opened the wet cover of her notebook and lifted out her limp history paper. The ink was smeared, making it totally unreadable. What would Ms. Novak say? You dummy, Amanda berated herself. Why can't you be more careful? And she loved books, too, and had always handled them with care. As she walked toward the entrance, she remembered her fifth birthday, one of her best. She had received five books, her favorite being a tall book of fairy tales, which had been breathtakingly illustrated. And now, because she hadn't paid attention to what she was doing, she'd ruined a book!

During history class Amanda delicately turned

the sodden pages of her bloated textbook, unable to read the blurred print. There was no way out. She'd have to confess to Ms. Novak.

After class, she took a deep breath and went up to the desk. "Ah, er, Ms. Novak, I — I . . ." She moved one foot in front of the other.

"Yes, Amanda?" Ms. Novak looked at her expectantly. "What is it?"

"I — well, I . . ." Without another word, she slowly brought out the book from behind her. "I set my book down in the snow and . . ." Helplessly she offered up the soaked book.

"Amanda!" Ms. Novak gasped, eyeing the saturated book. Delicately she took the expensive text with the stuck-together pages. "Do you know how much this book costs?"

Amanda thought. "No, I don't," she squeaked, "but I'm sorry." Hot tears trembled behind her lashes, but she gulped back the salty drops. "And — and, my paper got all wet, too."

"Don't worry about your paper. I'll give you an extension. But you'll need a replacement for your history book." She paused, examining Amanda's stricken face. "I'll have to ask you to pay for your ruined book."

"How much?" Amanda asked in a tiny voice.

"Eighteen dollars."

"Eighteen dollars!" Amanda blurted out. She didn't have eighteen dollars. How could one book cost so much? Ms. Novak didn't have to charge her the full amount. It was only because she despised her that she was doing this.

Not only did she have to serve three detentions, and rewrite her history paper, but she also had to pay eighteen dollars on top of it! She bit her underlip. "I don't have eighteen dollars."

"Then I'll have to call your mother," Ms. Novak said in a quiet tone. "There are some things we need to discuss, anyway."

Dumbfounded, Amanda stared at her teacher. She wouldn't call her mother, would she? What an awful, horrible, terrible, rotten person Ms. Novak was!

8

Seated at the kitchen table with Sam curled up in her lap, Amanda was doing her math when the phone rang. Her back went rigid, and she dug her fingers into Sam's long fur, causing a yowl of protest. "Sorry, Sam," she muttered. Her mother answered. After a few seconds, Amanda knew it was Ms. Novak by how slowly her mother sank into the wicker rocker and how solemn her face grew.

"No," Sarah Kingsley said, leaning back and crossing one jeans leg over the other. "I didn't know Amanda was performing magic tricks in your class." She listened for a moment, then said, "I'll send a check to school tomorrow, and I'll have a talk with Amanda." Her hazel eyes glanced reproachfully at her daughter. "Yes, Ms. Novak. I appreciate your call. Yes, I know she's not a bad girl, and I'm sure we can straighten this out. Good-bye, and thanks again." Quietly she rose and replaced the phone, turning to Amanda. "Why didn't you tell me you were in trouble with your teacher?" She ran her slim fingers through her short brown hair, giving Amanda a puzzled look.

"I thought things would get better," Amanda said, drumming her pencil on the table.

"I met Kathy Novak when you first enrolled, and she was such a nice young woman," Sarah Kingsley said. "She told me this was her first teaching job and how much she was enjoying it." She paced around the table. "It sounds as if you're taking some of the joy out of it for her, Amanda. What she lacks in experience she makes up for in eagerness. And what's more," she added, pushing her hair off of her forehead, "you're lucky to have such a bright, lovely teacher."

Amanda groaned at this remark. Some luck!

"You've always gotten along with your teachers," Sarah Kingsley went on, looking questioningly at Amanda. "What's wrong?"

Amanda pouted, shoving her math book aside. "Ms. Novak picks on me," she said, knowing she should be more honest than that.

"Oh?" Sarah's eyebrows rose. "Is she the one who ruined your history book?"

"No, but . . ."

"Is she the one who does magic tricks during class?"

"No, but . . ."

"Is she the one who broke a school rule by getting in a snowball fight?"

"No, but . . ."

"No 'buts' about it, Amanda," she said briskly. "I'm writing out a check for your book, but you're to pay back every penny."

"I don't have eighteen dollars," Amanda wailed.

"You'll give me a dollar every week out of your allowance, and when you get a baby-sitting job you can give me that, too."

"Mom!" she protested. "I need a new outfit for Jonathan's party."

"Sorry," Sarah said, pouring a cup of coffee. She settled herself across from Amanda, gazing at her steadily. Amanda looked down at Sam, kneading his neck fur. "I want you to try to be extra nice to Ms. Novak," Sarah Kingsley said. "Work hard and do what she tells you."

"I'll try," Amanda said, stroking Sam's fur faster and not looking at her mother.

"Do more than try, Amanda," she said firmly. "Otherwise we'll have to take drastic measures."

"Like what?" Amanda asked.

"Grounded indefinitely."

Astonished, her eyes flew to meet her mother's. Grounded! She couldn't mean it. Why, she hadn't been grounded since — since she was eight years old and had finger painted a mural on the wall of her room. And now she might be grounded again! Miserably she stared at her mother. She didn't want to miss Jonathan's party. She didn't want to give up Jessica, and Megan, and Heather, just when they'd become friends. "I'll pay for the book and get along with Ms. Novak," she murmured, thinking that it might kill her.

But for the next few days things between her and Ms. Novak were calm, at least on the surface. No open fireworks. She was pleased she was earning A's in history and that Ms. Novak included her in all class discussions. She still did magic tricks but was careful not to get caught.

Saturday night, dressed for Jonathan's party, she twirled about, pleased with her image. Even though she didn't have a new outfit, she didn't look half bad. Over a crimson plaid shirt with a white collar, she wore a dark green sweater that hung loosely over her jeans. She primped before the mirror, happy her shiny red hair softened her freckly face. Her green eyes sparkled. Perfect for a St. Patrick's Day party, she thought with an impish grin.

Amanda's father drove her and Jessica to the party, stopping before the Greenes' brick colonial house. "Mr. O'Connor will pick you up at ten-thirty," he explained, "so, girls, be ready."

"We will," Jessica said, jumping out of the car.

Arm in arm they went in, greeted by music and laughter coming from the basement room.

The party was great. Jonathan's mother served dips that were dyed green, of course, and chips. Amanda did a trick with metal rings plus several card tricks, loving the wild applause. Later, while they were eating cake and ice cream, the kids begged for more. Pleased to be the center of attention, Amanda did a mirror trick.

On the way home, she glowed with her success. Jessica turned to her. "You were terrific, Amanda."

"Thanks, Jessica," she replied softly. Never had popularity been this easy. So this was what she had to do to be well liked. All she had to do was keep performing new magic tricks and she'd please everyone! She couldn't wait to learn more magic from Philip.

Things continued to be outwardly peaceful in history. Amanda was pleased to be included in the crowd's activities, and Ms. Novak hadn't even punished her when she caught her doing the rope trick. However, when titters swept across the classroom, she did become upset. Lately Amanda had felt an undercurrent of restlessness and inattention in Ms. Novak's room. Oh, maybe she was partly responsible, but it wasn't her fault Ms. Novak couldn't control her own students.

On a sunny day in April, with the leaves budding out and the yellow jonquils nodding in the warm breeze, Amanda felt like singing. Only six more weeks of school and she'd be through with Ms. Novak forever!

When she entered the classroom, Jonathan was at the chalkboard map writing in all fifty states and their capitals.

"Ms. Ellinger is coming in today," he cheerfully reminded her while he filled in New York.

"Oh, yes, I almost forgot. Her supervisor is going to watch Ms. Novak teach." Amanda giggled. "Ms. Novak told us to be on our best behavior."

"That'll be hard for you, Amanda." He laughed.

"I've been very good," she said, bristling.

"Yes, you're like the little girl in that nursery rhyme," he teased. " 'When she was good, she was very, very good, and when she was bad she was horrid.' "

She ignored that remark, peering at the map instead. She marveled at the neat way he'd written in every eastern state, and had them in their correct places. Jonathan was a whiz at geography.

When the bell rang, Jonathan sat down, grinning at her. "When are you going to be horrid again, Amanda?"

Amanda sat down, too, not answering Jonathan's question. She wouldn't be tempted into doing anything silly. But when Ms. Ellinger, a tall, big-boned woman, stalked in and squeezed into one of the tiny back row desks, she suppressed a smile. Glancing at Jessica, they both broke into giggles, which sent ripples of laughter down the rows. Ms. Ellinger frowned, writing on her yellow pad. She did seem favorably impressed, however, when she studied the students' outline maps displayed on the bulletin board.

Smiling nervously, Ms. Novak stood before the class. She looked more dressed up than usual, wearing a pink linen suit, pearls, and high heels. Clearing her throat, she tugged at her jacket and asked the class to take out their books. Amanda felt a twinge of pity for her and vowed to be the perfect student. She wiped the smile off her face and stared straight ahead, hoping she wouldn't do anything to embarrass Ms. Novak. She remembered what her mother had said. Ms. Novak enjoyed teaching, but she was new at it. It couldn't be easy to have your boss watching every move you made. Especially with a class as wiggly as they were.

However, when Jonathan passed her a note, she couldn't resist opening it and peeking at the contents: *Do something funny.* She glanced at him, shaking her head. Then taking a pencil, she wrote, *You do something funny. I'm in enough trouble.*

She glanced back and saw Ms. Ellinger's terrible glare. Ms. Novak saw it, too, and immediately walked over to Amanda's desk. "Give me the note, Amanda," she demanded, holding out her hand.

9

When Ms. Novak stood over her, Amanda quickly did a little sleight of hand, crumpling up the note, and slipping it up her sleeve.

"Amanda," Ms. Novak repeated sternly. "Give me the note!"

Amanda turned her palms upward and gazed innocently at her teacher.

Flabbergasted, Ms. Novak stared down at Amanda's empty hands.

"Where is the note?" she asked in a low voice. "Give it to me at once!"

"I don't have it," Amanda replied, knowing the note was nestled against her arm.

Uneasily Ms. Novak glanced back at Ms. Ellinger who was again scribbling furiously. "I'll see you after class," Ms. Novak said ominously, her blue-gray eyes as dark as a stormy sky.

Amanda gave Jonathan a side glance. Why was she always the one to get caught? Jonathan was the one who had passed her the note and he hadn't even been scolded. It wasn't fair, she thought bitterly. It was just like on the playground! Others had been throwing snowballs, but she was the one who was caught red-handed. And today of all days when she wanted to be careful not to embarrass Ms. Novak, she was seen writing notes!

The rest of the lesson didn't go well for Ms. Novak. No one could answer any of her questions, and when time came to discuss the reading, she drew another blank. At last a few students responded, but they gave wrong information. The class was a flop! Ms. Novak, a faint flush on her pale cheeks, looked at the clock, unable to fill in the remaining time. "The last fifteen minutes you may use as a study period," she said lamely.

As soon as the class opened their books, Ms. Novak glanced hopelessly at Ms. Ellinger. The tall supervisor somberly pursed her lips and gathered up her papers. When she left, everyone breathed a sigh of relief, smiling at Ms. Novak.

But she didn't smile back. "Didn't anyone read today's assignment?" she questioned, removing her jacket and hanging it on the back of her chair. "I don't know what Ms. Ellinger thought. You're certainly better students than you showed yourselves to be today." Dejectedly she sat down, a few tendrils escaping her neatly combed hair. The class was so quiet you could have heard a bee buzz.

Amanda felt terrible. She wished she hadn't hidden the note. But without a note she couldn't be punished, and at the time that was all she had been able to think about.

After class she went up to Ms. Novak for her usual scolding.

"I know there was a note," Ms. Novak stated positively. "I saw it, and so did Ms. Ellinger!"

"Yes, there was," Amanda admitted, unable to deny the truth. "But when you asked for it, it wasn't in my hand." She felt a stab of guilt for deceiving her teacher.

"Where was it?" Ms. Novak asked evenly.

"Up my sleeve," Amanda replied in a small voice.

"You're just too clever for your own good, Amanda." Ms. Novak bit the tremor in her lower lip. "The very next time this happens I'm sending you to Mr. Brownley. I've had enough of your tricks and constant disruptions!"

Mr. Brownley! Amanda thought. No way did she want to tangle with the principal of Kennedy.

"Understood?" Ms. Novak said, and her forehead furrowed.

She seems tired, Amanda thought sympathetically, and even her crisp blouse looks rumpled. Amanda felt her face growing hot. She shouldn't have given Ms. Novak such a hard time. But no matter how good she tried to be, she always did something to upset the class, and half the time she didn't even mean to.

"Do you understand?" Ms. Novak repeated slowly.

"Yes, Ms. Novak." Amanda edged closer to the desk and cleared her dry throat. She wanted to tell Ms. Novak how sorry she was and that it wouldn't happen again, but the words stuck in her windpipe.

Opening her grade book, Ms. Novak put a mark by Amanda's name. "Your citizenship grade affects your history grade, you know It's too bad," she said with a sigh. "You're an A student, but you won't let yourself earn the grade you deserve . . . ." Her voice trailed off. "Next week you're to serve five afternoon detentions."

Amanda didn't even care about staying after school for an hour every day. She deserved to. She only wanted to make amends. Again she started to apologize. "Ms. Novak, I'm . . ."

"You're dismissed, Amanda." Ms. Novak held her head in her hand, rubbing her forehead.

"I — I wish I . . ."

"You're dismissed!" she said again, looking up at her sharply. "I don't want to hear any more of your excuses."

Amanda moved abruptly to the door, realizing

she'd never convince Ms. Novak that she could change. At least not today!

She served her week's detentions and even helped Ms. Novak grade tests. She yearned to talk to her and tell her what a good teacher she was, but Ms. Novak was cool and distant toward her. It was almost as if she thought she'd be contaminated if she talked to Amanda.

On the first day of May, Amanda was bent over the drinking fountain when she heard Ms. Novak talking to Ms. Emerson, Amanda's English teacher.

"I tell you, Marie, I just hate to confront my first period class," Ms. Novak said. "I used to enjoy them, but not anymore."

Horrified, Amanda glanced up at her two teachers. Fortunately they had their backs to her.

"You don't mean the class with Jessica, Jonathan, and Amanda, do you?" Marie Emerson asked.

"That's the class," Ms. Novak said grimly.

"But they're such darlings, Kathy."

"They were darlings first semester, but now all they do is giggle and act up. Ever since Amanda Kingsley entered Kennedy last January things have fallen apart."

"But Amanda has such a bubbling personality,"

protested Marie Emerson. "And she's very bright."

"Oh, she's bright all right!" Kathy Novak said bitterly. "Her very first day she corrected me on a date! She's smart and knows it! On the day Ms. Ellinger came in to observe, she just about finished me off! You should read the evaluation Ms. Ellinger wrote! She concluded her report by saying: 'Ms. Novak has a few discipline problems that interfere with her teaching.'

"Marie, I'm absolutely at my wit's end with Amanda. She's such a pain. She was passing notes that day! And Ms. Ellinger saw it!"

"Just be firm with Amanda!" Marie Emerson advised in a consoling tone.

"Oh, I try. I've given her detentions, called her mother, and talked to her. But Amanda goes right on doing magic tricks and getting into trouble. She's a constant cut-up."

Amanda leaned against a locker, her knees weakening. Kids streamed past her, yet all she noticed were blurred faces. To think Ms. Novak had called her "a pain."

"After Ms. Ellinger's write-up of my lesson," Ms. Novak went on, "I'm afraid I won't be rehired."

"Don't worry, Kathy," Marie Emerson said soothingly, putting her arm around her. "You've volunteered for extra assignments, the kids like you, the faculty likes you, and even old Brownley likes you. You'll be fine!"

Kathy Novak just shook her head. "No, Marie. After Ms. Ellinger's report, I'm dead."

"Nonsense!" Marie exclaimed. "Ms. Ellinger's retiring, and she won't be around next year."

"It's this year I'm worrying about."

Marie laughed. "Just go in there with fire in your eyes. You'll see. They're sweet kids and they'll shape up."

"Except Amanda."

"Amanda will, too. I know it."

"Thanks, Marie. I needed to talk to someone. I've really felt depressed after reading Ms. Ellinger's evaluation. Even Jim hasn't been able to cheer me up."

Jim must be Ms. Novak's fiancé, Amanda thought, walking away, her feet dragging. Poor Ms. Novak. First period for her must be like facing a den of lions! And Amanda Kingsley was the one with the sharpest teeth and the loudest roar!

Amanda turned and headed for history class. Ms. Novak was afraid she wouldn't be rehired. Amanda wished her heart would stop hammering. She and Ms. Novak had their differences, but she never dreamed she might be responsible for Ms. Novak losing her job! She swallowed, trying to get rid of the pain in her throat. How could she face Ms. Novak?

76

10

Even though Ms. Novak wasn't her favorite teacher, still Amanda didn't want to see her lose her job. But she couldn't talk to her mother about it. She wouldn't understand. Her mother blamed her already for every little thing that went wrong between her and Ms. Novak. She'd be grounded until she was eighteen! She decided to confide in Jessica. Maybe she'd have some advice.

She called Jessica and when she was invited to come over and bring her skates, it took Amanda only five minutes to sling her roller skates over her back and fly out the door. Breathless, she arrived at Jessica's and found her friend waiting for her on the front porch, going to and fro in the porch swing.

"Hi," Jessica said, running to meet her. "Let's skate over to Northwestern University."

"Sounds good," Amanda said. Sitting on a step, and fitting on her yellow roller skates, she began to tell Jessica about her school problem. "So, I'm

scared that I've caused Ms. Novak to lose her job."
She gave Jessica a sidelong glance, hoping she
wouldn't agree with her.

"All because of Ms. Ellinger's report?" Jessica
asked, her eyes big.

"That and a few other things. I know Ms. Novak
blames me for everything that's gone wrong in
first period." She strapped on her left skate.

"That's crazy," Jessica said. While waiting for
Amanda, she tottered upright on her skates and
did an uneven figure eight. "Just because you
make us laugh, Amanda, it doesn't mean you're
the only one in class who gives Ms. Novak fits."
She screeched to a stop. "If you go getting serious
on us, all the fun will stop, Amanda!"

Jessica was right, Amanda thought gloomily.
She'd created an image that she couldn't shake.
Sort of a Frankenstein monster that stalked her
like a giant shadow!

"Let's skate along the lakefront," Jessica said,
going ahead of Amanda.

For a moment Amanda stared after her. Jessica
hadn't really said a word that would solve her
dilemma. Maybe she didn't think Ms. Novak was
worth worrying about. Maybe, Amanda thought,
she was exaggerating the whole problem. Maybe
Ms. Novak was a rotten teacher and would have
lost her job whether she, Amanda, had come to
Kennedy or not. How could she, little Amanda

Kingsley, cause a teacher's dismissal? Amanda felt better. No doubt she was blowing up things way out of proportion.

The warm spring breeze blew her soft curls about her face, cooling her. Yes, she reassured herself, she wasn't responsible for Ms. Novak's future. She breathed a sigh of relief and laughed aloud. "Hey, Jessica," she shouted, skating faster, "wait for me!"

Bending low, with her arms swinging in front of her, she caught up with Jessica. Side by side they skated, one smooth leg stroke followed by another along the broad concrete lane that curved around the lakefront.

Stopping at a roadside vendor's truck for a soda, they skated over to a park bench to catch their breath. A blue jay hopped in front of them and paused, cocking a beady eye at them, then flew onto a limb of a nearby oak. The tiny leaves on the gently swaying branches resembled green lace against the bright turquoise sky. Amanda shifted her gaze from the cloudless sky to Lake Michigan's blue-green waves. Amanda enjoyed sitting quietly next to her best friend and listening to the lapping waters, the chirping birds, and the chattering squirrels.

"Why so quiet, Amanda?" Jessica questioned. "You're thinking about Ms. Novak, aren't you?"

Amanda nodded. "I'd almost convinced myself

I wasn't to blame for her losing her job, but I know I had *something* to do with it." She picked up a pebble and threw it into the lake. "Only a month left of school," she said with an impatient sigh of relief. "I can't wait."

"Me neither," Jessica said, smiling at Amanda. Then she turned to her in excitement. "Oh, Amanda, we'll have a great summer. My parents have rented a cottage at Lake Geneva. The week after school's out we're heading for Wisconsin for ten days. Mother said I could invite one girl-friend." She paused, her blue eyes twinkling. "Would you like to come with us?"

Amanda caught her breath. A week at a lake with Jessica! "Oh, I'd love to!" she answered eagerly.

"We'll swim, go to the movies in town, sun on the dock, and Dad will take us sailing. We leave two days after school's out." Jessica glanced at her, pushing back a long strand of hair. "Do you think your folks will let you come?"

"I'm positive," Amanda said. "Philip has already signed up for a month at Camp Echo." She laughed. "This will even things out. If Philip goes somewhere, my parents want me to have the same 'opportunity,' as they put it."

Jessica squeezed Amanda's arm. "We'll have a great time. Dad will take us to the amusement park, too. There's a roller coaster, a tilt-a-whirl, and the Spinning Devil. We'll ride everything! Even though we're a little old for the merry-go-round, we'll go on that, too. We'll have cookouts every night and maybe even go fishing!"

"Sounds terrific," Amanda said, already imagining the good times they'd have.

"Come on," Jessica said, pulling her up. "I'll race you to the lighthouse."

"You're on!" Amanda yelled and propelled herself forward, her skates whirring.

The afternoon with Jessica ended too soon, but somehow her day had brightened. It made her feel good to focus on the future, too. They'd talked about going into seventh grade at Nichols Junior High, an even bigger school than Kennedy. The thought of a new school didn't scare her as it once had. In fact, she was looking forward to it — especially to having a different history teacher.

At home Amanda headed right for the kitchen, opening the refrigerator. Her mother and father were huddled close together over a cup of coffee. She delighted in the way they looked at one another and talked everything over.

"Hi," Amanda said, pouring a glass of milk and setting the peanut butter jar on the counter.

"Hi, darling. What have you been up to?" Sarah Kingsley asked, her hazel eyes warm.

"Roller skating with Jessica down by the lake."

81

"Have fun?" Dad asked.

"Lots," she answered, reaching for the grape jelly.

"Don't spoil your dinner," her mom warned, taking a sip of coffee. "Amanda," she said gently, "I told your father about your problems with Ms. Novak."

Amanda stopped smearing peanut butter and jelly over a piece of bread, and looked sideways at her.

"Are you getting along any better with her?" Mr. Kingsley asked, pushing up his horn-rimmed glasses.

"A little," she said faintly, glad he wasn't angry. Yet she didn't really want to discuss Ms. Novak. Her parents didn't know that Ms. Novak might lose her job.

"Let me know when you want to talk about it," her dad said gently.

"I will," she replied. Maybe she should just sit down and tell them about what she'd overheard Ms. Novak and Ms. Emerson talking about. She was sure they'd understand. They usually did, although, she thought hesitatingly, her mother had blamed her for all the trouble with Ms. Novak, and she was still paying for that stupid history book. While Amanda was torn about whether to confide in them or not, her mother solved her problem.

"Paul," she said, placing her hand over her husband's. "We're due at the Bryants' in ten minutes."

"That's right," he said, rising.

"We won't be too late," Sarah said, blowing Amanda a kiss.

Reluctantly Amanda watched them leave, then looked back at the mess on the counter. Bread, jelly, peanut butter, and milk.

"Hi, little sister." Philip came in, grabbing the carton of milk and filling a glass. "I've got a great trick for you."

"You have?" she asked, taking the last bite of her sandwich. "What is it?"

Philip chuckled. "Not so fast." Above his hawk like nose, his close-set eyes gleamed. "It'll cost you."

Suspiciously Amanda narrowed her eyes. "How much?"

"A week's dishwashing."

"How do I know the trick is worth it?"

"Oh, it's worth it, all right," he said, and took a deep drink of milk. "You'll be able to make things disappear, like billfolds, pens, wristwatches — almost anything. Your hands will move faster than the blink of an eye." He waggled his fingers before her face.

She hesitated. What did she care about magic? She was through with all that.

"Well," he said, meeting her eyes. "What's it going to be?"

She grinned at him. "You've got a milk moustache under your beak."

With the back of his hand, he impatiently wiped off the white rim of milk. "Well," he growled. "I haven't got all day. Do you want to learn the trick or don't you?" He was not accustomed to her hesitation.

Not replying immediately, she put away the peanut butter jar. She didn't often get the chance to tease Philip. He always thought she'd jump to follow him in whatever he did. But little sister was growing up, she thought smugly, and big brother wasn't the sun, moon, and stars anymore. Just the sun. Nonetheless, she was curious about what he had up his sleeve — so to speak.

"Well?" he said, pulling out his key chain, and flipping the silver keys up and down. He smiled mysteriously. Suddenly the keys were gone.

Amanda's eyes and mouth grew round. She realized she didn't want to give up her magic. She couldn't! And, oh, wouldn't Jonathan and Jessica be impressed with a fantastic new trick! She made up her mind. She'd learn the trick! But, she promised herself, she'd never perform in Ms. Novak's room. Even before she smiled at Philip, he nodded knowingly as if he knew she'd say yes.

11

At school the next day Amanda came to history early and went directly to the Corner Book Nook. Choosing a book from the shelf, she settled herself into a big chair, propped up her feet on the footstool, and waited for Jonathan and Jessica. She smiled when she thought of Philip's sleight-of-hand trick and the way she'd mastered it. She'd practiced until she had become very agile and very good. She turned on the arc lamp and wriggled into the leather folds of the chair. She loved the Book Nook. Ms. Novak had arranged several big chairs, a round shag rug, a fish tank, and hanging plants to make this a very cozy place. She encouraged her students to come in early and use this nook to read.

Amanda couldn't keep her mind on her book. Where was everyone? She wished Jonathan and Jessica would hurry. She couldn't wait to try out her new magic trick. She knew she'd promised herself *not* to do any tricks in Ms. Novak's room, but she couldn't resist.

Shouting, Jessica, Megan, and Heather dashed in, covering their heads with their books. "William!" Heather screamed. "Stop it!"

William came flying after them. He aimed his squirt gun at Megan. "Where you running to?" he asked, fiendishly. "Scaredy-cats!"

"If you want to get something wet, squirt the fish!" Jessica said, perching on the arm of Amanda's chair. "They like water. We don't!"

William, his disheveled brown hair sticking up in all directions, moved closer to Megan.

"Don't you dare!" she yelled. "I'll tell Ms. Novak." Gasping for breath, she dropped into the rocker.

Jonathan entered the room. "Better not, William," he said, his face lighting up with a grin. "They've had enough."

William looked doubtful but backed away, shooting a stream of water into the fish tank. "I guess you're right," he said.

"Got any new magic, Amanda?" Jonathan asked, his brown eyes flashing.

She grinned, rising to her feet. She had dressed with care this morning, knowing she'd be the center of attention. Her green wool pants, her white-and-green-striped blouse, and her newly shampooed hair with a green ribbon above her ear made

Amanda feel pretty and gave her confidence. Nonchalantly she tested her shirt sleeve, then faced them with a smile. "Oh, I have a trick or two for you," she said, pleased that he'd asked. The Book Nook was the perfect background to show off her latest sleight of hand. Class hadn't started yet, so she wouldn't be doing anything wrong.

"Well," Jonathan said, lifting his black brows and tilting his head in her direction. "Give."

Standing before the fish tank, Amanda said in a solemn voice, "For starters, I'll eat a goldfish for you."

"Sure you will," William scoffed, folding his arms over his big chest. "If you eat a goldfish, I'll surrender my squirt gun."

"It's a deal," she said, giving him a cocky smile. "I've always wanted a squirt gun." Deftly she slipped a slender carrot wedge from her sleeve into her hand and plunged her hand into the tank, splashing the water. Wiggling the carrot back and forth, she brought it forth with a flourish. Suddenly she popped it into her mouth, swallowing it.

"Ugh!" Jessica said, making a face. "How could you eat a goldfish! What an awful thing to do!"

Amanda tried to keep her face immobile but had to grimace when the carrot stick stuck in her throat.

"Look!" Megan shouted, bouncing out of the

rocker, her short dark hair flying, "there's Moe, Joe, Flo, and Zorro. All four fish are still swimming around." She glanced at Amanda suspiciously. "You didn't eat a fish, did you, Amanda? What gives?"

"It's magic." Amanda shrugged. But a wild tickle in her throat was driving her crazy. She had to gulp hard to force the carrot down.

"Neat trick, Amanda," Jonathan said approvingly.

"Neat but nasty," Jessica added. "Do something where you don't eat anything, especially something alive!"

"She didn't eat a fish," exclaimed Heather. "Can't you count? All the goldfish are there!"

"Well," Jessica said with a sniff, "she ate something that looked like a goldfish."

"Any other new tricks?" Jonathan questioned.

Amanda cleared her throat, and the last of the carrot slid down. "I need an object," she said, looking about brightly. "Any object."

"Here!" Megan said. "Take my pen!"

Amanda took the black pen, waving a handkerchief over it. Moving rapidly, she let the pen fall into her left sleeve and immediately thrust her hand behind her. The index finger of her right hand poked up under the handkerchief, resembling the pen. She held up the handkerchief for everyone to see. Then with a gleeful shout, "Abra-cadabra," she whisked away the handkerchief, turning up her empty palms. "No pen!" she exclaimed with a wide smile.

"How'd you do that?" Heather asked. She began a hunt, peering under a chair and lifting the rug.

Jonathan felt around the lampshade and searched the bookshelf.

Amanda laughed, loving the puzzled looks everyone wore. "The pen's in plain sight. See if you can find it, Megan."

Megan narrowed her eyes. "Roll up your sleeves, Amanda."

Dutifully Amanda rolled up her sleeves. "Nothing up my sleeves except my arms," she said breezily, a glint of amusement in her eyes.

Megan flipped over the chair cushion but came up empty-handed. "I give up. Where's my pen?"

"I spy!" Jonathan exclaimed triumphantly.

"Where? Where?" Megan questioned, hurrying to his side.

"I'll give you a clue," he said with a chuckle. "Your pen's someplace where it's all wet."

"It's all — wet," Megan said fearfully, dreading to look at the only place it could be. Finally her eyes rolled toward the fish tank. "Oh, no," she moaned. "You threw it in with the fish, Amanda! How could you?" Folding up her sweater sleeve, she plunged her hand to the sandy bottom. "My good pen!" She groaned and brought up the dripping pen. Her round face screwed into a glare for Amanda. "You didn't have to get it soaked! I'll bet it doesn't even write!" With a stiff back she stalked off to her desk.

Heather gave Amanda a funny look and joined Megan.

Unmindful of Megan's annoyance, Amanda looked about. "I need one more object," she coaxed. "A small object." Her eyes fastened on Jessica's hand. "Give me your ring, Jessica."

Jessica shook her head violently. "This was my grandmother's opal ring. She had it reset for my birthday." Her blue eyes became stubborn. "I don't want it to end up in a smelly fish tank."

"It won't, I promise," Amanda answered, blowing away a red-gold strand of hair that tumbled across her forehead. She was ready to fool Jessica.

Reluctantly Jessica pulled off the ring. "Well, all right. But be careful! And hurry up. The bell's going to ring any minute."

Amanda smiled, relishing Jonathan's attentive look, William's big eyes, and Jessica's fidgety fingers.

Holding up the ring with the milky white stone sparkling in the sunlight, she wafted a scarf over it. "Hocus pocus!" she intoned, whipping off the scarf. Both hands were empty. The ring had disappeared.

Everyone stared, stupefied. "Where'd it go?" Jonathan asked.

William flattened his face against the fish tank. "Not in here," he said.

"It's up your sleeve," Jonathan guessed, intently watching Amanda.

"Yes," Jessica agreed. "Roll up your sleeve, Amanda."

The bell rang, and Ms. Novak entered. "Everyone sit down," she called out.

Amanda rolled up her left sleeve. "Nothing here," she said.

"Roll up your other sleeve!" Jessica commanded.

Amanda twirled about, ready to produce Jessica's ring with a flourish. But when she reached up her right sleeve, she couldn't put her hands on the ring. She bewilderedly patted her sleeve. But there was no ring. Panic rose in her throat. Where was it?

Expectantly Jessica held out her hand.

"Jessica, Amanda, William, and Jonathan. We're waiting for you to be seated," Ms. Novak said drily.

"Give me my ring," Jessica whispered harshly.

Amanda's smile faded. "I — I'll give it to you

later," she said, moistening her dry lips. She wondered what had happened to the ring. Something had gone wrong!

Jessica raised her chin. "You'd better find my ring in a hurry," she said in a menacing tone. Tossing back her hair, she gave Amanda a cold stare, then turned on her heel. Sinking into her desk she stared straight ahead.

Amanda huddled in her seat, feeling sick to her stomach.

12

For a stunned moment all Amanda could do was sit and stare at the hanging wall map and wonder where the opal ring had vanished to. If she had lost Jessica's ring, she'd also lose her best friend. But how could the ring just disappear? She'd held it in her hands! Don't panic, she thought, sucking in a deep breath. The ring had probably fallen out of her sleeve and was lying on the floor. When class was over she'd simply go over to the Book Nook and find it.

"And so," Ms. Novak concluded, her hands in her cardigan sweater's pockets, "tomorrow is the deadline for field trip money. I need an accurate count for the bus." As she talked, she walked quietly down the aisle, picked up the squirt gun off Amanda's desk, and without a word walked back to her own desk. As she slipped the gun in a drawer, she gave Amanda a reproachful glance.

William shot her a look of triumph as if to say, "OK, I lost the bet about the goldfish and had to give you my gun, but you won't get to use it!"

Amanda looked away, hating William's smirk. Another black mark on her record, she thought gloomily. And she hadn't even touched the gun! William had put it on her desk. Ms. Novak must think she was a hopeless pest!

"Only a few people haven't paid," Ms. Novak said. "Remember tomorrow is the last day!"

Amanda made a mental note to bring her three dollars in the morning. The year's end field trip to Chicago should be fun. She was looking forward to seeing the Chicago Historical Society and Lincoln Park. After they'd eaten their bag lunches in the park, Ms. Novak had promised that they could go to Lincoln Park Zoo. Amanda wasn't the only one who was excited. Jessica and Megan had been talking about it for weeks!

When the bell rang, Amanda scooted to the back of the room and began her hunt. She thought Jessica might have stopped to help her, but she stood with her arms folded. "Don't pretend my ring is lost, Amanda!" she said with a slight snicker. "You know exactly where it is!"

"Jessica, I don't," Amanda replied in a choked voice. "It's disappeared."

"Right," Jessica agreed, tilting her head to one side. "You and your phony tricks!"

"Jessica, magic tricks don't always work and . . ."

94

" 'And, and . . .' " Jessica mocked. "I don't want to hear anymore of your stupid excuses! You're a liar, Amanda!"

"I'll make it up to you, Jessica. I promise."

"Oh? All you have to do is return my ring!"

"I can't," Amanda protested weakly. "I feel terrible."

"How do you think I feel?" Jessica snapped. "That was my grandmother's ring! You'd better give it back to me." She glared at Amanda. "To think I called you my friend!" With these words she lifted her chin and walked away.

Sadly Amanda watched her leave. Well, she thought, once she'd found the ring, everything would be all right again. At first glance Amanda didn't see anything, so she began to look more closely. But the longer she searched, the heavier her heart pounded. The ring was nowhere in sight! Her palms grew sweaty. Surely she must be mistaken. The ring had to be here! It just had to be! Dropping on all fours, she crawled around, peering under chairs and around the fish tank. But the ring had disappeared.

"Ms. Novak," she said hesitantly, rising to her feet and dusting off her pant legs. "I — I lost an opal ring this morning, and it should be somewhere around here. I just can't locate it."

With concern Kathy Novak rose from her desk and said, "I'll keep my eyes open, and I'll tell Mr.

Bronson, the janitor, to watch for it, too." When she noticed Amanda's stricken face, her eyes warmed. "Maybe it was just misplaced. Was it valuable?"

"Yes, and it wasn't mine. It was Jessica's."

"How did you happen to have Jessica's ring?"

Amanda looked down at the floor, feeling her face burn. "It was a trick I learned, and . . ."

"And," Ms. Novak finished, in a resigned tone, "you lost Jessica's ring by practicing your never-ending magic. Is that what happened?"

"Yes, Ms. Novak," she answered miserably. She wished she didn't have to tell her, but she'd alert Mr. Bronson and he was her only hope of finding it. Certainly when he cleaned the room, it would turn up. Maybe someone had already taken it to the lost and found.

"I hope the ring is found, Amanda," Ms. Novak said sympathetically, turning away. Then she stopped. "Oh, by the way, if you want your squirt gun back, come in after school and I'll give it to you. But," she cautioned sternly, "you must promise that you won't bring it back to school."

"I promise," she mumbled, going out with her head down. Why should she bother to explain that it had been William's gun and that she'd only won it on a bet? Ms. Novak always thought the worst of her, anyway!

At the end of the day she raced back to check

with Ms. Novak, but the ring hadn't been found. The next morning she hurried to find Mr. Bronson, but he hadn't seen it, either. Next she ran to the front office to go through the lost-and-found box. She pawed through mittens, gloves, scarves, books, and keys, but the opal ring remained missing. Where, where, she wondered despairingly, could the ring have gone? She recalled the scene of Jessica, Jonathan, and William watching her trick with the ring. Could it have fallen and William pocketed it as a joke? No, not even blunt, brash William, who loved practical jokes, would do such a thing. He was too honest. He wouldn't have kept the ring this long, knowing the torture she and Jessica were going through. However, she was desperate and questioned both Jonathan and William, but neither one had any idea where the ring had disappeared to. At first they teased her; then, when they saw how miserable she was, they stopped and tried to reassure her that it would turn up. But as the day wore on and she kept searching and hunting and checking in different areas of the school, she came to the bitter realization that the ring was really gone.

On the following Wednesday, the day of the field trip, she went to the front office for one last time. Ms. Quinlan, the school secretary, shook her head sadly. "Sorry, Amanda, the ring hasn't shown up.

I keep hoping someone will bring it in, but no luck. I'm afraid it's lost."

Dejectedly Amanda went outside to wait for the school bus. Jessica and Megan had their heads together, giggling, but when they saw her, they pointedly turned their backs. Amanda felt a hard knot in her stomach. Was there no way to win Jessica back? She'd learned a new coin trick, and maybe at lunchtime she'd spring it on her. Jessica loved to be surprised, and this magic was guaranteed to make her laugh! But Amanda wasn't sure that was the answer. Jessica was *really* upset.

Jonathan came up behind and gave her hair a tug. "Got anything good to eat in that sack?"

She lifted her tote bag, grateful for his friendship. "Only a turkey sandwich, a candy bar, and an apple. And," she added with a grin, "it's all for me!"

"Hey, Amanda," William said, plodding forward, "did you ever find the ring?"

Leave it to William to remind her! Her heart plummeted as she nervously glanced at Jessica. "N-no, I haven't, William, but I'm sure it will turn up."

"Sure, it will," Jessica replied with false sweetness. "When you're good and ready to 'find' it!"

"I wish I had your ring," Amanda said wistfully. "I'd give it to you in a minute, Jessica. Do you really think I could do such a thing?"

"Yes, I do!" Jessica's eyes flashed with fury. "I thought I knew you, Amanda, but I was wrong! Fine friend you turned out to be! You stole my ring and I want it back!"

Amanda rigidly held her tears in check. Hopelessly she gazed into Jessica's eyes, which had darkened to a thundercloud-blue. Deep down Amanda knew the ring was gone for good. And so was Jessica.

13

On the way to the Chicago Historical Society, Amanda sat alone on the bus. Across the aisle Jonathan and William were jostling and shoving each other, while Jessica, Heather, and Megan whispered in the back. Amanda was certain they were discussing the lost opal ring. She'd wracked her brain wondering where it could be, but she had no idea.

Before the bus arrived at the museum, Ms. Novak handed each student a worksheet. "These questions are to be answered at the numbered exhibits," she explained. "I want you to pay particular attention to the room where Lincoln lay dying after he was shot. They've done a remarkable reproduction of the room in Washington D.C., where he was carried."

She adjusted the polka-dot scarf at her throat and continued, "When we move on to the Chicago Fire Exhibit, read the explanations on the glass cases, and everyone fill out their own answers!"

She smiled, her long-lashed eyes shimmering with a bluish luster. Amanda studied her neat, trim teacher in a different light. When she wasn't mad at her, she didn't seem like such a bad teacher after all. She even wished she looked more like Ms. Novak. She admired her small, straight nose, rosy complexion, and wide mouth in an oval, rather delicate face. Amanda Kingsley would never be a glamour girl, she thought with a crooked little smile, although her new, softer hairstyle had earned her a few compliments. She'd even been stared at by an eighth-grade boy, all of which didn't mean anything without any friends. She glanced at Jonathan and William, who, in a way, were her friends, but she couldn't really talk to them and their teasing drove her crazy. With a sigh, she turned her attention back to her teacher.

"The questions aren't hard and won't take you long," Ms. Novak said reassuringly. "Please hand them to me before we leave the museum." She reached over and ruffled Jonathan's springy hair. "It's a beautiful day, and I want every one of you to have a good time." The bus jolted to a stop, and she had to grasp the back of a seat to keep her balance. Everyone giggled, and so did she. "Stay together and follow me," she instructed, still chuckling. "And mind our two chaperons." She waved a forefinger at them, but her tone was light. "Ms. Rollins, Megan's mother, is a parent chaperon, who's following the bus in her own car. She'll join us at the museum entrance." She indicated Mr. Poindexter, who sat in a front seat. "Mr. Poindexter is our second chaperon." The teacher leaped up, placing two fingers to his high forehead in a snappy salute and grinned. Everyone clapped and cheered for their popular science teacher.

Staring out the bus window, Amanda, with folded arms, sat in lonely silence, observing the big red brick building with the tall white columns. All her classmates were enjoying themselves except her. She wondered who she'd eat lunch with!

When the class tumbled out of the bus and ran up the steps, however, Amanda jingled the coins in her jeans pocket and smiled secretly. That was one thing her parents had taught her. There was always a bright side to every blue feeling. And today, despite losing the ring, she would try to win Jessica back. And when she'd regained Jessica's friendship, Heather and Megan would soon follow.

Entering the museum, Amanda trailed closely behind Jessica. When the blonde girl whirled about and said, "Megan . . . ," she stopped in midsentence when she saw Amanda. Pressing her lips together, Jessica gave her a chilly look, then hurried forward to catch Megan. Grabbing Megan's arm, she began to chatter about how lovely Lake Geneva was. "You'll *love* it up there, Megan," she said, putting her arm around her.

"Oh, I can't wait," Megan responded eagerly.

Obviously, Amanda thought unhappily, this was Jessica's not-so-subtle way of telling her that she was no longer invited for the week at Lake Geneva. And she had been so ecstatic about it, too. Her optimistic mood evaporated completely.

After a brief film on the exhibits, the class circulated among the displays. For a few glum moments Amanda watched her former friends clustered together, then moved ahead by herself. Soon she became engrossed in seeing Lincoln's tall stovepipe hat, his cane, and watch. Walking on, she paused at the replica of the room in which the President had died. The bed was so short, and he was so tall, she thought in dismay. The chair nearby was where Mary Todd Lincoln had sat weeping for her wounded husband. A kerosene lamp and Lincoln's eyeglasses were on a side table. Quickly she filled in the answers on her worksheet.

The history of the Chicago fire was fascinating, too. Over one hundred years before, the fire had raged across the city, burning out of control. Over one third of Chicago had been destroyed. Amanda stopped to examine the nineteenth-century firemen's gear. Axes, helmets, long coats, and clumsy rubber boots had been their uniform. A bright red fire engine, pulled by four wooden horses, was displayed in the center of the room. Amanda became so intent on studying the shiny brass bell and the big spoke wheels that she almost forgot she wasn't one of the group.

When Amanda had completed and handed in her worksheet, she emerged into the sunlight, the warmth hitting her full force, along with the nagging question, Who would she have lunch with? Then she remembered her coin trick. After she had performed this slick piece of magic, maybe Jessica would know Amanda was doing it just for her, to try to make Jessica feel better. Then Jessica would forgive her and ask her to join them.

Benches and tables were spaced along a blue lagoon surrounded by weeping willows. The sunlight filtered between the drooping branches, casting dancing shadows on the moss-covered water. Along the bank, a mother goose led four waddling goslings. What an ideal spot for a picnic!

"Hey! Gang! Come and get it!" Mr. Poindexter shouted, carrying a case of Coke. "You're allowed one can." He set the case down on a picnic table, then dodged the eager reaching hands.

"Ms. Novak, if there's any left over," William coaxed, "can I have it?"

"Yes," Ms. Novak said with a laugh, "you *may* have an extra one, William."

"Everyone spread out," Mr. Poindexter ordered. "Eat your lunch, and at one o'clock we'll hike over to the zoo."

Shouts of "Yeah!" and "Hurrah!" filled the air. This was the highlight of the field trip. Amanda couldn't wait to see the zoo, which had recently been redone with each animal in its own natural habitat. A baby panda had been born and the class had a special invitation to visit the Baby Zoo. Except it wasn't much fun to go alone.

"The lion feeding is at two o'clock, then at three-thirty the bus leaves. Everyone please stay together," Ms. Novak said. She joined Jessica and Heather and Megan, chatting with them briefly. Then, passing Amanda she gave her shoulder a friendly pat. Amanda glanced up gratefully, watching Ms. Novak rejoin Mr. Poindexter and Ms. Rollins. Megan's mother was spreading out the lunch.

Amanda moved out to the lagoon's edge, away from the three adults. She didn't want Ms. Novak to scold her for performing magic, but on such a sunny day and with Ms. Novak in such a good mood, she might even join in the fun.

"Hey! Everyone!" Amanda shouted, taking out two quarters, and clinking them together. "I have two quarters that I can change into four."

Jonathan was instantly alert. "Go for it, Amanda. Show us how that can be done. If you can double our money you'll be busy all day!" He laughed, taking a big bite out of his ham sandwich.

Encouraged by his laughter and William's, too, she stepped closer. "Watch this!" she said dramatically, holding up the silver quarters so that they glittered in the sun. She glanced at Jessica, who'd raised her head and was studying Amanda between narrow eyes. Amanda was elated. Jessica was interested! Maybe she could rekindle their old friendship.

Clicking the quarters together, she stood up tall and said in a deep voice, "I'll now prove the hand is quicker than the eye!" Smiling, she held up each quarter. "Observe closely!" she said in a commanding voice. With a rapid movement, she whipped out a scarf from her pocket and took a step backward. Suddenly she found herself falling, falling. She clawed at the air, latching onto a low tree limb, which snapped in her hand. As she plunged downward, waving a puny willow twig, she screamed, "H-Help! H-e-e-l-l-p!" But brackish lagoon water filled her mouth, closing over her head.

14

Down, down Amanda plunged into the murky depths of the lagoon. Long tendrils of algae wafted around her face as she struggled to stand. At last her feet touched the soft silt bottom. Seaweed wrapped around her ankles, and her lungs were ready to explode. Desperate for air, she waved her arms up and down like fish flippers and propelled herself to the top.

Bursting through the moss-covered surface, she gulped in huge mouthfuls of oxygen. Her ragged gasps tore at her throat, and she tottered halfway forward, then halfway backward, trying to keep her balance. Much to her astonishment, she discovered she was standing upright. When she'd first fallen in, she must have hit a hole. She wasn't going to drown after all, especially not in a lagoon only waist deep. Even though it was a sunny day in May the lagoon was still frigid, and the icy water penetrated to her bones. With numbed fingers, she scooped back her plastered hair, staring directly at the class lined along the shore.

Ms. Novak, her brows drawn together in an agonized expression, stood on the bank. "Keep calm, Amanda. We'll get you out."

But Jonathan had already slid down to the lagoon's edge, holding out his hand. "Amanda! Grab my hand!" he commanded, his dark eyes steady as if he knew exactly what he was doing.

Thankfully she grasped his hand and moved out of the mud, which sucked at her feet. Plop! Plop! She lifted first one foot, then the other. Ugh, she could imagine the crawly things beneath the swampy surface, like fat slimy leeches. She tried to hurry, but she floundered, the mud holding her back. She teetered backward, slipping out of Jonathan's grip. Desperately she tried to reach his outstretched hand.

"Hold on!" Jonathan yelled, his face red and puckered with effort, as his fingers once again laced with hers.

Splashing forward, Amanda firmly clutched his hand with both of hers and staggered out of the lagoon amidst shouts and calls. She must look like the Dripping Green Monster from the Green Slime Lagoon, she thought. Shivering, she collapsed on the ground, letting her fingers curl lovingly on solid ground. Never had land felt so wonderful.

"Oh, dear," Ms. Rollins said nervously. "I have two blankets in the trunk of my car. I'll get them.

Oh, I almost forgot. I have my gym bag in there, too, with a sweatsuit."

"Meet us at the shelter house, Ms. Rollins," Ms. Novak said hastily, her face lined with worry. She looked down at Amanda. "The first thing we'll do, Amanda, is get you out of those wet clothes and wrap you in blankets."

Mr. Poindexter hurried forward, unscrewing his thermos. "I still have some hot coffee left." He forced the hot liquid between her chattering teeth. "You'll be all right, Amanda," he said with a comforting smile, "even if your lips are blue."

Trembling, Amanda lay back, exhausted. She opened one eye to peer at the faces gazing down at her. Hadn't they ever seen an algae-covered girl before? She smiled weakly. But no one smiled back. What an idiot she'd been. All because of a stupid magic trick!

William's face twisted in a grimace. "Does this mean we don't get to go to the zoo?" he asked in disgust.

"The class will go on to the zoo with Mr. Poindexter," Ms. Novak answered. "Ms. Rollins and I will take Amanda home."

Amanda jerked to her feet, coughing and sputtering. "I'm better, honest I am." She had looked forward too long to this field trip and didn't want to give it up.

"No, Amanda," Ms. Novak said in a controlled

tone. "We need to get you home as soon as possible. Can you walk?"

"Y-yes," she uttered in a choked voice, wondering how she could have made such a fool of herself.

"Then come with me to the shelter," Ms. Novak said. "Everyone else will stay with Mr. Poindexter. He'll be with you the rest of the afternoon."

Amanda tugged at her hair, drawing out a piece of dripping seaweed. She glanced around for Jonathan who stood by an oak, busily wiping off his shoes on the grass.

"My new sneakers," he muttered, giving her a dark look.

"Jonathan, thanks," she said, between heaving breaths. "You saved my life!"

"In two feet of water?" he asked with a thin, mocking smile, then went back to cleaning his shoes. He shrugged at the hopeless task. "Look at my sneakers!" he growled, shaking his head.

"I'm sorry about your shoes, Jonathan," she said in a husky voice punctuated by a coughing fit.

"Amanda, you're nuts!" he said shortly.

A few mumbles and mutterings greeted her as she meekly followed Ms. Novak. No one thought she was funny today, not even with water squishing out of her shoes.

"She's always messing things up," she heard

Jessica say. Others murmured in agreement. She coughed again, feeling cold and wretched. She'd ruined the day for herself, for Ms. Novak, and for Ms. Rollins. She was hopeless!

Accompanying Ms. Novak to the shelter house, she wrung out her shirttail on the way. Ms. Novak, her chin high, didn't say a word.

Undressing, she wiggled into Ms. Rollins's sweatsuit. The sleeves dangled a foot below her hands, and the pant legs had to be rolled up six times. Even then, she felt like JoJo the Clown as she stumbled after Ms. Novak and Ms. Rollins on the way to the car.

Wrapped in blankets, she huddled in the corner of the backseat. The end of the field trip had been a fiasco! As soon as Ms. Novak was assured she was all right, her good mood vanished. Amanda peeked at her sitting in the front seat next to Ms. Rollins, but she no longer wore her bright smile.

Ms. Novak turned around. "After the school nurse has examined you, Amanda, I'll call your mother and take you home."

"Do you have to call my mother?" Amanda asked in a tearful voice.

"Of course. Your spill could have been serious. And we don't want you to catch pneumonia."

Amanda shuddered, but not from her cold dunking. She stared out the window as they drove along Lake Shore Drive. Lake Michigan was an azure blue today with fluffy white clouds suspended overhead. Bikers pedaled along the bike path and a few sailboats glided near the shore. The scene should have made her feel good, but it only made her feel worse. About now, the kids were seeing the baby panda or watching the lions devour their lunch. A tear slid down her cheek.

When they arrived at school, Ms. Rollins drove away, and Ms. Novak ushered Amanda into the nurse's office.

After a checkup, the nurse pronounced her healthy and fit, and dismissed her with a few words of advice about staying away from lagoons. Ms. Novak heartily agreed, then drove Amanda home.

"Amanda," she said, a slight break in her voice, "you've disrupted the class field trip with your thoughtlessness. Mr. Poindexter is left with the entire group to chaperon, which isn't fair."

"I'm sorry," Amanda said, wiping her nose with one hand and hugging her bundle of damp clothes to her chest with the other.

"You should be!" She glanced disapprovingly at Amanda. "I phoned your mother, and she'll be at home when we get there. She had to miss a very important meeting." A swift shadow of anger crossed her face. "Every chance you get, Amanda, you're showing off. See how much trouble it gets you into?" she accused. "I don't think you'll ever learn!"

Amanda slumped lower, barely able to see out the window. All she could glimpse were treetops rushing past. Ms. Novak was driving very fast. Probably wanted to get rid of her as soon as possible.

Ms. Novak applied the brakes, screeching to a stop. She faced Amanda and said, "I must report your accident to Mr. Brownley. I don't know what disciplinary action he'll take, but I've decided not to punish you. You've gone through enough today." Her eyes flashed with silver lights. "But Amanda, if you try any more magic in my room you'll be serving after school detentions for the rest of the year!"

Amanda flinched. Could things get any worse? she wondered painfully. What would the principal do? Mr. Brownley always appeared stern and unsmiling.

The next day Amanda returned to school, feeling and looking much better. The night before she'd had a warm bath, washed her hair, and gone to bed early, sleeping ten solid hours. And her parents hadn't been too hard on her, either, considering what she'd done.

On Friday when she entered Ms. Novak's class,

her friends, *former* friends, she corrected, were gathered by the fish tank. She pasted a smile on her face, determined to make up for her past bad behavior. She'd apologize and ask for another chance. From now on things would be different.

All at once Jonathan dipped into the fish tank, pulling out a piece of seaweed. "Who does this remind you of?" he asked, throwing his head back with a laugh.

"Looks like 'Seaweed Amanda' to me," William said, grabbing the dripping green weed and waving it in front of Megan.

Megan drew back in disgust.

"Seaweed Amanda!" Heather said, nodding her head approvingly. "That's a good name for her! She almost ruined our field trip. What a jerky clown!"

Amanda froze, unable to force her legs forward.

"Seaweed Amanda," Jessica said, rolling the words around on her tongue. "That fits Amanda perfectly. Seaweed." She wrinkled her nose. "Ick! And who likes seaweed?"

"Ugh! Not me!" Megan said, grabbing the small weed from William and tossing it into the fish tank. She gave him a haughty look, then faced Jessica. "She never did return your opal ring, did she?"

"No, I don't know where she's hidden it!" Jessica said forcefully, gathering up her books.

114

"I haven't hidden it," Amanda said firmly, stepping forward.

Surprised, Jessica turned, confronting Amanda. "Then where is it?" she snapped.

"It will turn up, I know it will." Amanda answered miserably.

Jessica's eyes snapped blue sparks. "It'd better!" She turned away, adding in a voice taut with anger, "And I thought you were my friend!"

Amanda's throat closed, suffocating her. She *was* Jessica's friend, but the only way she could prove it was to find the ring, and right now that seemed pretty hopeless. And the awful nickname they'd tagged her with! "Seaweed Amanda." Jessica's words pounded in her ears: "And who likes seaweed?"

Amanda spun around and dashed out.

15

On Sunday Amanda sat by her bedroom window with Sam on her lap. As she brushed his long fur faster and faster, she felt sorrier and sorrier for herself. She was more lonesome than when she'd first come to Evanston. "I don't know, Sam," she said softly, petting his back. "I've lost all my friends." Even Jonathan was disgusted with her, she thought sadly, remembering how he'd tried to clean off his muddy sneakers.

Maybe she could win her friends back, but how? She'd overheard herself being called a "jerky clown," "Seaweed Amanda," and Jessica had said she was always messing things up. "And you know what, Sam?" she asked her cat in a trembling voice. "Jessica's right! No matter what I do, I cause trouble." Ms. Novak had said so, too! And what could she do to make Jessica believe that she wasn't hiding her ring? She'd searched every place — even in the fish tank.

She brushed Sam's orange striped fur until it

gleamed like polished copper. Rolling over, head hanging down, Sam began to purr. Hugging Sam to her, she whispered, "Sam, Sam, I worked so hard to win friends here, and now I've lost them all!" And Ms. Novak might even lose her job because of her. But what could she do? The more she tried to be friends with her teacher, the more they didn't get along. There was no explaining it. Every time they were together the sparks flew. "I guess, Sam, there are just some people you can't get along with in this world. The smart thing to do is keep away from them." It wasn't easy, though, when that person was your teacher and had control of your life — at least as long as you were in the sixth grade.

Sarah Kingsley came into Amanda's bedroom, her hazel eyes sparkling. A few strands of hair escaped from the red bandanna she'd tied around her head. "Dad's got the station wagon packed, and it's a beautiful day." She had rolled up her cutoffs and the sleeves on her oversized top. "Are you ready, Amanda?"

"I'm ready," she said, giving Sam a gentle nudge. The cat jumped lightly down and stalked away, tail high. She should be happy that the family was going on a picnic today, but somehow it didn't thrill her. She and Philip had been encouraged to invite a friend, but she'd told Mom that she didn't feel like it. Her mother had looked at her strangely but thankfully hadn't asked any questions. It was plain to see, though, that the phone had stopped ringing and that her girlfriends didn't want anything to do with her.

As soon as they arrived at the beach, Mr. Kingsley set up the grill and Sarah Kingsley spread out the checkered tablecloth on a picnic table near the water.

"Want some help, Mom?" Amanda volunteered, trying to keep a cheerful smile on her face. She'd guessed that the reason for the picnic was because she'd been dragging around all weekend.

"No, dear, you run along. The boys are over by the pier. You might learn some new magic."

"Thanks, Mom," she said, moving away. She carried a box of stationery, preferring to write to Ann. Learning more magic would only get her into deeper trouble.

Passing Philip and Ian, she paused to watch them toss three metal rings back and forth.

"Hey, want to learn how to juggle these rings?" Philip called, a large silver ring flashing in his hand.

"Sure, come on over," Ian echoed. "Philip says you're pretty good with your hands. You can be our assistant."

"No, thanks," Amanda said with a weak smile. As she walked on, she noticed the magic equipment they'd spread out on a table: scarves, cards, coins, ropes, and mirrors.

Reluctantly she tore herself away and strolled along the shore. When she discovered a sheltered cove beneath the branches of a gnarled old oak, she settled down on the fine white sand. Taking off her sandals, she curled her toes in the warm grains and gazed out at the whitecaps ruffling across the emerald lake. It was funny how the lake changed. The water could be blue one day and green the next. She'd even seen it a dull gray and a brilliant turquoise. Suddenly a motorboat roared by with a water skier hanging on behind. His skiis slapped up and down, and maneuvered over the waves like a rider on a bucking bronco. He was dressed in a wet suit, for the water was still frigid. Amanda shivered at the memory of her cold plunge into the lagoon.

Briefly she closed her eyes, leaning against the tree trunk and letting the gentle breeze blow through her hair and caress her face. Spring was wonderful with the soft promise of lazy summer days ahead. School would soon be out, and she'd have three months to play. Then with a sudden stab of regret she thought of Lake Geneva. She and Jessica would have had such fun. But that was before she'd lost her opal ring. Now Megan was going in her place.

Well, she still had Ann, who had always been a true friend. Too bad she was so far away. Maybe this summer her folks would let her go back to Iowa for a visit. She'd love to see Ann. They used to have such fun at the river. They'd skitter and slide down Oak Hill and lie on the boulders jutting out over the water. She hoped it wouldn't be like last summer when they had to scare away the water snakes, but they wanted a place to sun on the flat rocks, too. She didn't much like swimming with them, either. She could still see their heads poking out of the water like little sticks.

A sailboat bobbed by and Amanda shook her head. She'd better stop daydreaming about Ann and the river or she'd never get her letter written. She propped her stationery box against her knee and began:

May 17

Dear Ann,

> *I miss you something awful. I can't wait until school is out. I'm going to ask if I can visit you. Won't we have fun going shopping at the mall? I hope you're going to be home. Evanston is the pits. I met some nice kids but we ran into all*

120

kinds of trouble. Like I lost Jessica's ring, so now she's not speaking to me. It makes me feel awful! On top of it all, Ms. Novak and I are still fighting. She's even worse than our kindergarten teacher, Ms. Dreblow. Remember when I couldn't fold my May basket? She kept me after school until I'd folded fifteen of them. My mom finally came to school looking for me. It was past five.

Philip is his usual bratty self, so I can't depend on him to do anything. Besides, he's got lots of friends. Ian, especially. In fact, I'm on a picnic now, and the two guys are practicing their magic. (Magic has got me in trouble at school.) Take Thursday, for instance. Our grade was on a field trip, and I fell in the lagoon. I got drenched in cold water, and the kids got mad at me. I had to come back to school, but the class went on to the zoo. But enough about me and my problems. What are you up to? Does Ms. Worthington still wear that purple dress every other day? Now that I'm gone, I'll bet things in class are better. We never could look at each other without cracking up.

Well, I'd better stop. I hear Dad yell-

121

*ing to come and get it! I hope I can visit
you next month. Let me know.*

      Love and a hug,
      Amanda

For the next few days Amanda worked hard
and got along fairly well. She missed Jonathan's
and William's teasing and wondered if they were
going to be forever mad at her. During the first
period, Ms. Novak had given the class a study
time and didn't mind if they talked to one another
quietly. Amanda didn't feel like opening her textbook. Her heart ached when she sat at her desk,
listening to the whispers around her. Was she to
be shut out forever just because she'd made one
little mistake?

She glanced sideways at Jonathan. He didn't
seem mad at her. But it was as if he didn't know
she existed. Forgetting her promise of no magic,
ever, in Ms. Novak's room, she decided to try to
make friends with Jonathan, not knowing how
he'd take it. She reached over and whispered
shakily, "What's this, Jonathan?" And she pulled
a nickel from his mouth. William let out a hoot.
She pulled another nickel from his right ear and
a third nickel from his left. Ms. Novak stopped
writing on the blackboard and turned in time to
see Amanda flip a nickel in the air. Jonathan

grinned and Amanda grinned back. His cocky smile gave her a warm glow inside.

"Amanda Kingsley! I'll see you after class!" Ms. Novak said in a discouraged voice.

Surprised, Amanda glanced up but only answered meekly, "Yes, Ms. Novak." She heard Jessica giggle, but it didn't bother her. Jonathan had smiled at her. That was all that mattered. At least he wasn't mad at her any longer. It was worth a detention or two just to see Jonathan's old grin.

After class Ms. Novak assigned her three detentions but didn't lecture her. It was as if she'd given up.

When school was out, Amanda went to her locker with a springier step than she'd had in days. She didn't care about three detentions. She had regained a friend. If she could win over Jonathan, maybe she could win over Jessica. It was worth a try. Removing her books from the top shelf, she discovered her history notebook was missing. She must have left it in Ms. Novak's class.

Hurrying back to room 111, Amanda stopped in the doorway, her breath catching in her throat. Ms. Novak was at her desk and she was crying.

"M-Ms. Novak . . ." she stammered, standing awkwardly first on one foot, then on the other. She didn't know what to say.

When Kathy Novak looked up and saw

123

Amanda, she hastily wiped her red eyes and turned her head.

Embarrassed, Amanda's face burned. She didn't know whether to go or stay. She'd never seen a teacher cry before! What should she do?

16

Amanda almost walked on tiptoe to her desk, not wanting to disturb Ms. Novak. Even though she'd dried her eyes and busied herself with desk papers, Amanda could tell she was still upset. Picking up her notebook, Amanda pretended she didn't notice anything was wrong, but when she heard Ms. Novak sniffle, she couldn't stand it. She whirled about and said anxiously, "Ms. Novak, is there anything I can do?" Her tremulous voice wavered a little as she waited for an answer.

For a moment Ms. Novak remained quite still, her pretty face all red and blotchy. A tremor touched her lips. "There's nothing you can do, Amanda. I believe," she said evenly, "you've done quite enough. Because of you I received a bad evaluation when my supervisor visited my classroom. You remember Ms. Ellinger's visit, don't you?"

A warm flush stained Amanda's cheeks. How could she forget?

"Also, because of you," she went on, "the field trip was a disaster."

"But — but, Ms. Novak," Amanda argued. "I couldn't help it." She flung out one hand in a small gesture of protest.

"No, you couldn't help many things, Amanda. And, I suppose, this morning you had to perform your magic tricks just one more time, despite," she added, her brows drawing together, "all your promises."

"I — I hadn't meant to, but . . .," She hesitated. Didn't Ms. Novak realize she was miserable, too? Didn't she know she'd lost Jessica, her best friend? But how could she explain any of this to Ms. Novak? Her teacher never had been able to understand her.

"Furthermore," Ms. Novak said, "you've lost Jessica's valuable ring, and Mrs. O'Connor called again today to see if it had been turned in."

Amanda's eyes grew big. Now Mrs. O'Connor was added to her list of troubles. Was there no end to this nightmare? She stumbled backward. "I — I just thought I'd ask if I could . . ." She choked, as if she'd swallowed a hot coal.

"You'll be pleased to know," the young teacher continued, rising and looking out the window, "that I have a conference with Mr. Brownley and

Ms. Ellinger tomorrow afternoon. I don't think you'll need to worry about seeing much more of me, Amanda." Folding her arms, she confronted Amanda with a steady gaze.

Amanda wished she hadn't come back for her notebook. She should have known better. "You — you won't be around?" she asked, her voice trembling.

Sadly Kathy Novak lifted her violet cardigan from the back of her chair and threw it over her slender shoulders. The deep lavender changed her eyes to a smoky blue, and her voice grew husky. "After my meeting, I'm sure I'll be leaving Kennedy for good."

Horrified, Amanda stared at her with widening eyes. Had she caused all this?

As if reading her mind, Ms. Novak walked over and smoothed back Amanda's hair. "I shouldn't have blamed you, Amanda. It's just that I'm upset." She rubbed her forehead. "I've been wrong at times, too," she said with a half-smile. "It's not your fault." She moved to the blackboard and began erasing the day's assignment. "You run along, Amanda," she said in a soft voice, not turning around. "Don't worry."

Dejectedly Amanda left. Don't worry? How could she help *not* worrying? That's all she'd done lately! But this was the worst mess of all!

That night she helped her mother with supper,

recopied a short story for English, and went to bed without being told.

For a long while she lay staring out the window at the silver moon and a few winking stars. She wished she could ride a space ship into that dark sky, and never come back. Her lungs ached, and she could scarcely breathe. Even though Kathy Novak hadn't blamed her, she knew she was guilty.

All at once she sat up in bed. She knew what to do! First thing in the morning she'd go in and see Mr. Brownley. She'd tell him all the terrible things she'd done and how it was all her fault that Ms. Novak taught a bad lesson on the day that Ms. Ellinger was there. If she could save Ms. Novak's job, she didn't care how Mr. Brownley punished her. He could even keep her from participating in Play Day, the celebration of the last day of school. Just thinking of a plan to help Ms. Novak made her feel better. She took a deep breath, and snuggled down beneath her blanket.

The next morning she rushed through breakfast and was off before anyone could ask her why she was in such a hurry.

Racing into the main office, Amanda gasped, "I must see Mr. Brownley right away."

Wordlessly the astonished secretary opened the principal's door.

Mr. Brownley, a big man, was hunched over his desk, but when he saw Amanda, he nodded at her, indicating a chair. Smiling briefly, he said in a brisk tone, "What can I do for you, Amanda?"

Her mouth formed a small O. She was surprised that he knew who she was. But knowing Ms. Novak, she'd probably complained about her a zillion times.

"You're the girl from Iowa, aren't you?" He peered at her above his frameless glasses. "I was in Ms. Loomis's office when you registered."

"Oh, yes," she answered, pleased that Ms. Novak hadn't tattled on her after all.

Mr. Brownley raised his bushy eyebrows, expectantly examining Amanda's face.

Amanda cleared her throat, not knowing how to begin. But when she did, her words gushed out in a torrent. "Mr. Brownley, I came to tell you that Ms. Novak is a good teacher. All the kids in the sixth grade like her." She didn't tell him how *she* felt about her. "She's real helpful and the day that Ms. Ellinger came in, I — I, . . ." Amanda gulped, hating to admit what she'd done, but she boldly continued, "I was writing notes, and Ms. Novak asked for the note I'd been writing." She wavered and her voice caught. "I hid it up my sleeve."

"I see," the principal said soberly, stroking his chin.

"And Ms. Novak is nice, too," Amanda continued uneasily. She wished he'd smile again. "She planned a wonderful field trip for us last week, but I ruined everything when I fell in the lagoon."

"You did?" He moved his swivel chair in a half-circle one way, then the other. "Go on, Amanda."

"I'm always causing trouble. And I just don't want you to fire Ms. Novak because of me." She looked down at her thin fingers, twisting in her lap.

Suddenly Mr. Brownley roared with a laugh that shook the room.

Startled, she looked at him, wondering if he'd gone crazy.

"Amanda," he said, taking off his glasses and wiping his eyes. "Ms. Novak's going to be around Kennedy for a long time. She's one of our best teachers. Not once has she dumped her discipline problems in my lap. She's handled a very lively group of sixth-graders and handled them well." He put on his glasses once more. "No, no, never would the school board let Ms. Novak go. She's always volunteering for extra duties and committee work. I wish we had more teachers like her."

He rose and came around his desk. "You go on to your first period class, Amanda. Don't be concerned about Ms. Novak. And," he warned, wagging a plump finger under her nose, "don't pass any more notes!"

She rose quickly, her heart lifting. "Oh, I won't, sir." She moved to the door, turning the knob. "And thanks!"

Amanda was delighted as she went into room 111. Mr. Brownley was a real human being. She'd like to tell Ms. Novak that she still had her job, but she'd better let her find out for herself. She was elated, though, that she hadn't caused her teacher to lose her position. Why, she thought with a warm feeling, Ms. Novak hadn't even told Mr. Brownley about her. She really was a good teacher, she thought.

Suddenly Jessica came in and stood by the fish tank, eyeing Amanda. Her look wasn't really too unfriendly, Amanda thought. With a timid smile, she approached Jessica. Amanda touched the green silk tie around her neck, realizing it'd be perfect for a disappearing scarf trick she knew. Maybe it was just the thing to show Jessica. Maybe it was just the thing to bring them together.

Amanda glanced at Ms. Novak, who was seated at her desk, talking to William. She wondered if she dared one more magic trick. She'd won Jonathan back by magic, hadn't she? All at once she made a decision. She had to do the same with Jessica, even if Ms. Novak got angry.

"Jessica," she said, untying the mint-green bow at her throat. "I've got something to show you."

Jessica gazed at her, a gleam of interest in her big blue eyes. "You have?" she asked doubtfully.

Amanda could see she was curious about what she intended to do with the scarf. "You're going to love this."

For a moment Jessica inclined her head, then took a step forward.

Amanda smiled, too, folding her scarf in a square. But suddenly she couldn't make her stiff fingers move. Mixed feelings swirled within her. Then something clicked in her mind. She knew she couldn't perform any magic in Ms. Novak's class. Not any more. With quiet resolve, she quickly replaced her scarf at her throat and retied the bow. Staring helplessly at Jessica, she mumbled, "Maybe later."

Jessica gave her a bewildered look. Then, tossing her head, she gave an impatient shrug and retorted tartly, "The only thing you can show me, Amanda Kingsley, is my opal ring." She turned and stalked to her desk.

"Jessica," Amanda said, her voice fading. She'd really blown her chance with Jessica. Crestfallen, Amanda turned away.

17

On her way to Old Orchard Mall, Amanda rode faster when she passed Jessica's big white house. She was glad her former friend wasn't around. Pedaling along the curved avenue, she slackened her pace so that she could enjoy the colorful Victorian houses on such a warm, sunny Saturday afternoon. When she reached the lake bike path, several little boys dashed in front of her to reach the beach. Seeing a couple strolling along the beach, she all at once recognized Ms. Novak's petite figure and shiny chestnut hair. Amanda stopped, straddling her bike's crossbar to watch the man and woman arm-in-arm. They wore rolled-up jeans, and were barefoot, kicking at the sand as they walked. She heard Ms. Novak's laughter over the lapping waves. Maybe her teacher was warmer than she thought. Watching Ms. Novak having fun at the beach with her fiancé, Amanda wished she could feel some of that warmth! She gave a long, shaky sigh, remounted her bike, and pushed off. If only she had someone to talk to — like she used to with Jessica! She felt her face grow hot. Were those days gone forever?

As she approached the shopping mall with the gold banners flying, she wondered if Jessica and the gang were there having a good time.

Her mother had asked her to pick up a purse she'd put aside at Marshall Field's and gave her money for a Coke and the Orchard Art Fair, but she didn't feel like buying anything.

The maple trees surrounding the outdoor mall had leafed out with lime-green buds. Beds of bright red and yellow tulips lined the walkway, and in the distance the Patio Cafe, its tables topped with jaunty blue, green, and pink umbrellas, was filled with customers.

Amanda padlocked her bike to the wrought-iron rack, and headed for the small pond in the center of the mall. Several swans glided along the smooth water. Crossing the Japanese-style wooden bridge, she glimpsed goldfish flashing in and out among the lily pads.

Nearing Field's, Amanda stopped. There was Jessica coming toward her. She was all golden in a pale yellow T-shirt with her blonde hair flying. Did she dare say anything? Amanda swallowed, but the tightness in her throat remained. "Jessica," she called, but she needn't have worried about an answer. Jessica deliberately veered off in the opposite direction!

Moisture burned behind her eyelids as she watched Jessica's retreating back. Was Jessica so eager to get away from her that she almost broke into a run? Tears blinded Amanda as she hurried to Field's and pushed around the revolving door. Wasn't Jessica ever going to forgive her?

In bed that evening as she read a mystery she had to go back and reread the same paragraph over and over. She couldn't concentrate. She could still see Jessica avoiding her! And all because she'd lost her opal ring. Didn't Jessica realize she hadn't done it on purpose? Frustrated, she made a fist and beat her pillow. Sure, she thought sourly, she could do magic tricks, but this was the first time she'd ever made anything disappear into thin air! Life was no fun without Jessica! She longed to pick up the phone and call her, but what was the point? She didn't want the receiver slammed down in her ear! Miserably she turned out the light, and closed her eyes.

Somehow she got through the empty weekend, and on Monday afternoon when her mother asked her to get her woolen clothes ready for the cleaners, she was glad to have something to do. Megan and her family were unexpectedly going on a trip to California. Maybe, Amanda thought hopefully, Jessica would be as lonely as she was. But Jessica still had Heather. Besides, she was leaving for the lake next week. Since Megan couldn't go to the lake, she wondered if Jessica had invited Heather instead. One thing was sure, *she* wouldn't be going! Amanda flung her slacks and skirts on the bed, wishing it were next September and school was starting. In seventh grade she'd have a chance to make new friends. But the thought didn't console her. She and Jessica had gotten along so well, and she didn't want to find someone else.

Glumly she folded up her skirts, then held up her green wool pants by the bottom. All at once something fell out of the cuff, bounced across the room, and rolled under the bed. What was that, she wondered. A button? A penny? Getting down on her hands and knees, she lifted the dust ruffle and peered into the darkness. Something glistened in the corner. Puzzled, she reached for the shiny object. Suddenly she let out a wild whoop of astonishment. Jessica's opal ring had been found!

Dumbfounded, Amanda stared at the delicate ring. To think it had fallen in the cuff of her wool pants! No wonder it had disappeared into thin air. Who would have dreamed where it had been hiding? She laughed aloud, relieved to at last hold the elusive ring in her hand!

"Moth-er!" she crowed. When there was no answer, she pounded down the steps. "I found Jessica's ring!" she shouted, racing into the kitchen and waving the ring above her head.

When Sarah Kingsley caught sight of her daughter's wild excitement, she turned off the blender and wiped her hands on her jeans. "You found the ring?" she questioned in surprise.

"Yes, yes, I found Jessica's ring!" Amanda repeated, grinning and holding out the white translucent stone.

"Oh, Amanda! How wonderful." Sarah laughed and touched the beautiful gem. "Where was it?"

"In the cuff of my green pants," she explained, her eyes dancing. "I've got to call Jessica!"

"Why don't you just run over there?" Sarah said, one eyebrow tilting upward.

"I'm afraid Jessica won't let me in," Amanda said, half joking and half serious.

"Call, then," Sarah said, reaching for the wall phone and handing it to Amanda. She smoothed down her daughter's hair and touched her forehead to Amanda's. "This should bring back my old, happy Amanda," she said gently.

Amanda looked at her mother gratefully. So, she thought, dialing Jessica's number, even though she'd tried to hide her unhappiness, her mother had known. Mom always knew. She should have confided in her a long time ago. No wonder she'd promised her a trip to Iowa without a murmur!

Mrs. O'Connor's voice startled her.

"Hello. Mrs. O'Connor?" Amanda said into the receiver. "Is Jessica there?" She smiled, anticipating how glad Jessica would be.

When Jessica answered, Amanda's voice shook with happiness. "Jessica, it's Amanda. I found—"

But Jessica cut her off. "I don't want to talk to you!" she snapped.

"Jessica, wait!" Amanda said in a choked voice.

The receiver clicked in Amanda's ear. The line went dead. In dismay, she stared at the phone, then slowly replaced it. She dropped in a kitchen chair and gulped, trying to wet her dry throat. All at once she felt a ripple of apprehension shoot up her spine. Maybe even the ring couldn't restore their old friendship.

Sarah Kingsley tilted her head sympathetically. "What are you going to do?" she asked.

Dejectedly Amanda shook her head. "I don't know," she mumbled, feeling as if her breath had been cut off. She glanced at her mother, then suddenly jumped to her feet. "I'm going over there!"

"Good for you," Sarah said with a smile, watching Amanda race out the door.

Knocking on the O'Connors' double door, Amanda's heart thumped wildly.

Jessica opened the door. "Oh, it's you," she growled, glaring at Amanda. "What do you want?" she asked between clenched teeth, her hands resting on her hips.

In answer, Amanda held up the ring, its translucent whiteness sparkling in the sun.

Jessica jerked to attention, and gasped at the sight of the gleaming ring. "My opal!" she exclaimed, her eyes widening. She stared at her ring, then glowered at Amanda, her face hardening. "You had it all this time!" Furiously she snatched the ring from Amanda. "You're no friend!"

Speechless, Amanda met Jessica's blazing eyes. Her palms became sticky. Did Jessica really think she'd kept her ring on purpose? A breeze blew a few wisps of hair across her eyes and she impatiently brushed them aside. For a second all she heard was a scolding squirrel. Was Jessica just going to let her stand there? "Jessica," she said in a small tight voice. "I just found it a few minutes ago."

"Ha! And my name's Peter Rabbit!" Jessica replied sarcastically, her lips thinning angrily.

139

"What made you decide to finally return it?" Her accusing tone was edged with ice.

Amanda, standing motionless on the porch, found her voice and managed to stammer, "I told you, Jessica. I just found it." Hesitantly she smiled. "You'll never believe where it was."

"I'm sure I wouldn't believe *you*," Jessica retorted sharply, tossing back her hair. But clearly her curiosity overcame her. "Where was it?" Her sapphire-blue eyes narrowed as she warily studied Amanda's face.

"In the cuff of my wool pants," Amanda said, chuckling nervously. "I wouldn't have found it except Mom asked me to get my winter clothes ready for the cleaners. It fell out of my pant leg and rolled under the bed."

"Oh, sure!" Jessica said. "That's *some* story." She stared at Amanda. "You deliberately kept my ring all this time. I don't know why you did it, Amanda." She bristled with indignation. "I thought you were my friend."

"Oh, Jessica," Amanda said, flinging out her hands in an imploring gesture. "I *am* your friend. Don't you know that?"

"You have a funny way of treating a friend!" Jessica retorted harshly.

Amanda drew a deep breath. "I didn't hide your ring," she explained softly. "I didn't know where it was, either, Jessica. Honest. You have to believe me."

"I suppose my opal just appeared out of thin air," Jessica said, shaking her head in disbelief.

"Remember the magic trick?" Amanda said. "I hid the ring up my sleeve, and when I shook it the ring never appeared. I couldn't figure it out. I searched every inch of the classroom and checked the lost and found every day. And," she added shyly, "I've been saving fifty cents every week from my allowance to buy you a new ring." Moisture trembled on her eyelashes. "No one knew, not even my mom." What more could she say to make Jessica understand? "The last thing in the world that I wanted was to lose your friendship," she whispered in a strangled voice. Wretchedly she kept her eyes fastened on Jessica's angry frown. The silence lengthened between them, making her uncomfortable. Finally she whispered, "I'd never hurt you, Jessica." A teardrop slid down her cheek.

Jessica's blue eyes warmed. "We-l-l," she said, spacing her words far apart, "I guess you wouldn't really hurt me." All at once she smiled. "I'd never hurt you, either." She leaped up and moved quickly to Amanda's side. "I guess we've both been a couple of airheads! Think of all the time

141

we've wasted by being mad at each other." She grinned. "Besides, you'd go broke if you'd have to buy an opal! You'd be in debt until you were ninety!"

"I know." Amanda laughed shakily and brushed away a tear.

"We're leaving for the lake on Thursday," Jessica said, her face lighting up in an eager smile. "Do you still think you could come with us?"

Amanda nodded, her throat so tight she couldn't speak.

"Oh, you nut," Jessica said with the old giggle. "I can't believe my lovely ring was in your pant cuff all these weeks!" She flung her arms around Amanda. "I've missed you so!"

Amanda hugged Jessica tight, almost afraid to let go. Was it only a few hours ago that she'd wished for September and the beginning of school? She sniffled happily. Now she didn't care if school ever started. What a wonderful summer lay ahead!

"But," Jessica warned, breaking away and looking at Amanda sternly. "No more tricks or I'll throw you into the lake!" Her eyes were wet and glistening, too.

Amanda attempted a grin, but it was more like a lopsided grimace. "No more tricks," she promised. Silently she vowed that never again would she act the cut-up just to attract attention. Anyway, she didn't need to do that anymore. She had her old friend back! And if anyone begged for a magic trick, she'd simply smile and tell them she'd forgotten how to be a magician!

18

The last week of school for Amanda was great. She and Jessica had a lot of catching up to do. Jonathan and William teased her like always, and Heather and Megan were once more her friends. Life was beautiful again. Because of her successful conference with Mr. Brownley and Ms. Ellinger, Ms. Novak looked very happy these days. Amanda was glad she hadn't lost her job, but if it came to a choice between having your teacher happy or your best friend happy, it was no contest. Having the return of Jessica's sweet friendship meant everything to her!

Amanda's spirits soared when she thought of her summer. She was going to the lake with Jessica and soon would visit Ann. The whole summer would be fun! She was looking forward to seventh grade, too. She'd have a new beginning. A *right* beginning. Her magic tricks had petered out, and somehow she no longer wanted to win friends that way. So what if she proved that the hand was quicker than the eye? It might be entertaining for a while, but after she'd finished, then what? No, next year, she vowed, things would be different. She wouldn't be the class fool any longer! People would have to like her for what she was. Just plain old Amanda Kingsley with nothing up her sleeve!

The last day of school all the students took part in Play Day. It was fun, but Amanda was glad when the marathon races were finished and the last hot dog had been eaten and the last Coke had been drunk. Now it was time to go home. Home for the summer! As she went into the building, the halls were empty and she quickly cleaned out her locker. She'd removed most of her things the day before, but she still needed to peel off a poster. She smiled a little when she took down a small gift box from the top shelf. Ms. Novak would be pleased.

Closing her locker, she turned so abruptly that she bumped into Megan.

"Oh, hi, Megan," she said with a smile. "How's everything?"

Megan nodded. "Fine," she answered breezily. "Our volleyball team won today." All at once she smiled.

"Your braces are gone!" Amanda said in blank amazement.

"Yesterday," Megan said, her old grin returning and lighting up her dark eyes.

"You look great," Amanda said. "Your teeth are so even and white."

"You should have seen my teeth in fourth grade. They used to call me 'gopher mouth.' " She bared her teeth.

Amanda nodded with approval. "They look great," she repeated. "My bottom teeth are crooked." She stuck out her lower jaw, showing two overlapping teeth. "And Dad said I might need braces. Does it hurt?"

"Not too bad," Megan admitted.

"Hi, you two," Jessica said, coming up to them. "I just came from the baseball diamond." She gave Amanda a particularly warm smile. Even wearing sweats, she looked lovely, Amanda thought. She was pleased how quickly they'd been able to slip into their old, easy relationship.

"Oh," Jessica said, spying the small box. "Who's the present for?"

"Ms. Novak," Amanda answered. "They're beads. I figured I owed her after all the trouble I caused."

Jessica grinned. "I'd love to see her face."

"Wait for me," Amanda said, "and I'll tell you all about it."

Megan laughed. "You're always up to something, Amanda."

"We'll be out in front," Jessica said. "Maybe your peace offering will do some good."

146

With a chuckle and a wave, Amanda hurried down the hall to 111. She touched the present in her pocket, imagining Ms. Novak's surprise.

She was still smiling when she met Mr. Poindexter, carrying a cardboard box loaded with books. "See you in September, Amanda," he said jovially as he passed her. "Have fun."

"Thanks," she answered, waving. "You have a good time, too, Mr. Poindexter."

"Oh, we'll have a great summer!" he called. "The trailer's packed, and we're leaving for Wisconsin in the morning!"

Amanda hurried on, hoping Ms. Novak hadn't left.

But Ms. Novak was still there, stacking textbooks on the closet shelves. "Hi, Amanda," she said, piling one book on top of another. "They're waxing the floor this summer, so all books and materials have to be stored."

The south wind blew through the open windows, touching Amanda's cheeks, but the wind was too warm to cool her. Amanda stared in dismay at the stacks of books, the globe, a heap of magazines, a box of supplies, a pile of colored paper, and in the corner a set of rolled-up maps. Ms. Novak wouldn't get out of here until six o'clock, she thought.

She bit her lip indecisively. Then, making up her mind, she set down her books and rolled up her sleeves. "What can I do?" she asked.

Kathy Novak straightened. Her oval face, smudged with chalk dust, broke into a weary smile. She pushed back her flyaway hair and wiped her flushed face with the inside of her sleeve. "Those three piles of books need to be lined up on the lower shelf." Then she added, "Each class set needs to be counted." She studied her as if not believing Amanda was serious.

"Okay," Amanda said breezily, lifting a stack of books, and carrying them to the closet. Once the volumes were in a row, she began to count.

An hour later, on her knees, Kathy Novak picked up scattered papers and a torn notebook, throwing them into the wastebasket. Sitting back on her haunches, she moistened her dry lips. "Whew," she said, fatigue lines along her forehead. "I think we're finished." She rose, and Amanda admired her slender figure clad in jeans and a navy sweatshirt. She remembered how she'd once mistaken Ms. Novak for a student and today she looked like a teenager again.

"Now," Kathy Novak said, moving to her desk, "I only need to clear out a few more things and I can go home!"

She pulled out the middle desk drawer and began to sort out pencils, pens, paper clips, and staples. "I appreciate your help, Amanda. Now

I'll be able to keep a dinner date." She gave Amanda a radiant smile.

"That's okay," Amanda replied.

Holding a stapler in her hand, Kathy Novak gave Amanda a sidelong glance. "Mr. Brownley told me about your visit to his office." She paused. "I — I really didn't expect you to do such a sweet thing."

Amanda shrugged, coloring fiercely at the unexpected praise. She was pleased, yet a little embarrassed. "It was the least I could do after all the trouble I caused," she murmured. Suddenly she fished in her pocket and drew out the small box. "Here," she said, thrusting the gift at Ms. Novak.

Staring in amazement at the box, then at Amanda, Ms. Novak said softly, "For me?"

"For you," Amanda said with a grin.

Untying the ribbon, Kathy Novak opened the box, and lifted out a string of green beads. "They're lovely!" she exclaimed, her eyes sparkling with delight.

Without a moment's hesitation, Kathy Novak fastened them around her neck, and although the fancy beads looked strange on her sweatshirt, they were strikingly beautiful next to her smooth skin.

"I'm glad you like them," Amanda said, shifting

her gaze away from Ms. Novak's obvious pleasure. Quite a change, she thought, from the looks she usually got from her. "Well, I'd better go," Amanda said, feeling awkward and taking a step backward.

"Come here," Kathy Novak ordered gently, holding out her arms.

Feeling a stain of scarlet steal over her face, Amanda moved closer. Ms. Novak suddenly clasped her in her arms and gave her a big hug. Amanda loved the sweet violet scent of her teacher but couldn't believe she was actually in her arms. Tears stung her eyes but she swallowed hard and disentangled herself, not wanting to get too mushy. "The — the beads look pretty," she stammered, not knowing what else to say. Still, she gloried in this moment.

"I need to see these beads," Kathy Novak said eagerly, opening the closet door and looking in the mirror. For an instant she stared in bewilderment at her reflection, her fingers touching her bare neck. "The beads," she faltered. "Wh-where. . . ?"

"Is this what you're looking for?" Amanda teased, a flash of humor lighting her face. She dangled the string of green beads before her, unable to resist finding out if Ms. Novak could still take a joke.

"Amanda!" Kathy Novak chided, reaching for the delicate strand. "You're still cutting up, aren't you?" But laughter twinkled in her slate-blue eyes.

"Guess so," Amanda agreed with a slight smile. She picked up her books, ready to go. She was hot and sweaty and wanted to meet Jessica and Heather. Besides, she wanted to leave while she still had this good feeling about Ms. Novak.

"You have a good year in seventh grade, Amanda," Ms. Novak said. "One thing, though," and there was a trace of laughter in her voice. "Concentrate on your studies, and forget the magic!"

Amanda smiled. "Oh, I will." She held up two fingers, Girl Scout fashion. "Promise." She hesitated, then said boldly, "I'll miss our run-ins, though."

Kathy Novak smiled, her even teeth white against her dust-streaked face. "What did you choose for an elective in seventh grade?"

"Creative writing."

Kathy Novak picked up her briefcase, then slowly set it down again. "Creative writing?" she asked in a low, weak voice.

Amanda nodded, puzzled by her reaction.

"I'm teaching that course next year," Kathy Novak said, dropping in her chair.

"Y-you're what?" Amanda whispered.

"I'm teaching creative writing," Ms. Novak repeated.

Oh, no, Amanda thought, panic rising in her throat. She'd gotten along with Ms. Novak today, but could she take her for another whole year? A heaviness settled in her chest.

She met Ms. Novak's steady gaze, and all she heard was the swishing of the janitor's mop in the hall.

Ms. Novak rose. With a sigh of submission, she said, "We'll just have to make the best of each other." She gazed at Amanda, an amused glint in her eye. "So," she said in disbelieving wonder, "you'll be in my class again." All at once she gave a low throaty chuckle which erupted into a ripple of mirth. Finally she threw back her head and let out a burst of laughter.

Stunned, Amanda stared at her, then she, too, felt a giggle well up inside. Soon the two rocked back and forth, laughing uproariously. Howls of laughter reverberated throughout the room.

At last Kathy Novak, tears running down her face, leaned weakly against her desk and held her side. "Oh, Amanda," she gasped, trying to catch her breath. "It's so ironic!"

Amanda nodded uncertainly. She didn't know what ironic meant but it was probably like a funny coincidence.

"We'll both have to make a strong effort," Ms. Novak said, having regained her composure, "so that our relationship can work. I'm willing, if you are."

Amanda, still smiling, nodded. "I'm willing." And she was. She knew it wouldn't be easy, but she'd try. Eyes shining, Amanda looked warmly at her teacher. "Well, I'll see you next September, Ms. Novak," she said, and with a wave she went out the door.

As she walked down the hall and out of the building, her heart fluttered nervously. Just because they'd hugged today, she had no guarantee they'd get along next year.

Jessica and Megan rushed up to her.

"What happened?" Megan asked. "You were in there forever!"

"Did she like the beads?" Jessica said.

"She loved the beads."

"You look funny, Amanda," Megan said. "Anything wrong?"

"Maybe yes, maybe no." She shrugged her slender shoulders slightly. "Ms. Novak's teaching my creative writing course next year," she said uncertainly.

Jessica stared at her. "You're kidding! Ms. Novak will be your teacher again?" she questioned in disbelief.

Amanda nodded. "All year."

Jessica laughed, throwing her arm around her. "You'll get along. Don't worry."

Amanda attempted a smile. "I'm sure we will." At any rate, she was ready to meet Ms. Novak halfway. Maybe they'd both learned something this year. Slipping her arms around Megan and Jessica she glanced at them, smiling tremulously.

Jessica laughed and the three girls stepped lightly down the sidewalk toward Sycamore Street.

America's Favorite Series

THE BABY-SITTERS CLUB®

by Ann M. Martin

Collect Them All!

The seven girls at Stoneybrook Middle School get into all kinds of adventures...with school, boys, and, of course, baby-sitting!